NEVER FORGET

(A May Moore Suspense Thriller—Book Eight)

BLAKE PIERCE

Blake Pierce

Blake Pierce is the USA Today bestselling author of the RILEY PAGE mystery series, which includes seventeen books. Blake Pierce is also the author of the MACKENZIE WHITE mystery series, comprising fourteen books; of the AVERY BLACK mystery series, comprising six books; of the KERI LOCKE mystery series, comprising five books; of the MAKING OF RILEY PAIGE mystery series, comprising six books; of the KATE WISE mystery series, comprising seven books; of the CHLOE FINE psychological suspense mystery, comprising six books; of the JESSIE HUNT psychological suspense thriller series, comprising twenty six books; of the AU PAIR psychological suspense thriller series, comprising three books; of the ZOE PRIME mystery series, comprising six books; of the ADELE SHARP mystery series, comprising sixteen books, of the EUROPEAN VOYAGE cozy mystery series, comprising six books; of the new LAURA FROST FBI suspense thriller, comprising eleven books (and counting); of the new ELLA DARK FBI suspense thriller, comprising fourteen books (and counting); of the A YEAR IN EUROPE cozy mystery series, comprising nine books, of the AVA GOLD mystery series, comprising six books (and counting); of the RACHEL GIFT mystery series, comprising ten books (and counting); of the VALERIE LAW mystery series, comprising nine books (and counting); of the PAIGE KING mystery series, comprising eight books (and counting); of the MAY MOORE mystery series, comprising eleven books (and counting); the CORA SHIELDS mystery series, comprising five books (and counting); and of the NICKY LYONS mystery series, comprising five books (and counting).

An avid reader and lifelong fan of the mystery and thriller genres, Blake loves to hear from you, so please feel free to visit www.blakepierceauthor.com to learn more and stay in touch.

ISBN: 978-1-0943-7979-1

BOOKS BY BLAKE PIERCE

NICKY LYONS MYSTERY SERIES
ALL MINE (Book #1)
ALL HIS (Book #2)
ALL HE SEES (Book #3)
ALL ALONE (Book #4)
ALL FOR ONE (Book #5)

CORA SHIELDS MYSTERY SERIES
UNDONE (Book #1)
UNWANTED (Book #2)
UNHINGED (Book #3)
UNSAID (Book #4)
UNGLUED (Book #5)

MAY MOORE SUSPENSE THRILLER
NEVER RUN (Book #1)
NEVER TELL (Book #2)
NEVER LIVE (Book #3)
NEVER HIDE (Book #4)
NEVER FORGIVE (Book #5)
NEVER AGAIN (Book #6)
NEVER LOOK BACK (Book #7)
NEVER FORGET (Book #8)
NEVER LET GO (Book #9)
NEVER PRETEND (Book #10)
NEVER HESITATE (Book #11)

PAIGE KING MYSTERY SERIES
THE GIRL HE PINED (Book #1)
THE GIRL HE CHOSE (Book #2)
THE GIRL HE TOOK (Book #3)
THE GIRL HE WISHED (Book #4)
THE GIRL HE CROWNED (Book #5)
THE GIRL HE WATCHED (Book #6)
THE GIRL HE WANTED (Book #7)

THE GIRL HE CLAIMED (Book #8)

VALERIE LAW MYSTERY SERIES
NO MERCY (Book #1)
NO PITY (Book #2)
NO FEAR (Book #3)
NO SLEEP (Book #4)
NO QUARTER (Book #5)
NO CHANCE (Book #6)
NO REFUGE (Book #7)
NO GRACE (Book #8)
NO ESCAPE (Book #9)

RACHEL GIFT MYSTERY SERIES
HER LAST WISH (Book #1)
HER LAST CHANCE (Book #2)
HER LAST HOPE (Book #3)
HER LAST FEAR (Book #4)
HER LAST CHOICE (Book #5)
HER LAST BREATH (Book #6)
HER LAST MISTAKE (Book #7)
HER LAST DESIRE (Book #8)
HER LAST REGRET (Book #9)
HER LAST HOUR (Book #10)

AVA GOLD MYSTERY SERIES
CITY OF PREY (Book #1)
CITY OF FEAR (Book #2)
CITY OF BONES (Book #3)
CITY OF GHOSTS (Book #4)
CITY OF DEATH (Book #5)
CITY OF VICE (Book #6)

A YEAR IN EUROPE
A MURDER IN PARIS (Book #1)
DEATH IN FLORENCE (Book #2)
VENGEANCE IN VIENNA (Book #3)
A FATALITY IN SPAIN (Book #4)

ELLA DARK FBI SUSPENSE THRILLER
GIRL, ALONE (Book #1)

GIRL, TAKEN (Book #2)
GIRL, HUNTED (Book #3)
GIRL, SILENCED (Book #4)
GIRL, VANISHED (Book 5)
GIRL ERASED (Book #6)
GIRL, FORSAKEN (Book #7)
GIRL, TRAPPED (Book #8)
GIRL, EXPENDABLE (Book #9)
GIRL, ESCAPED (Book #10)
GIRL, HIS (Book #11)
GIRL, LURED (Book #12)
GIRL, MISSING (Book #13)
GIRL, UNKNOWN (Book #14)

LAURA FROST FBI SUSPENSE THRILLER
ALREADY GONE (Book #1)
ALREADY SEEN (Book #2)
ALREADY TRAPPED (Book #3)
ALREADY MISSING (Book #4)
ALREADY DEAD (Book #5)
ALREADY TAKEN (Book #6)
ALREADY CHOSEN (Book #7)
ALREADY LOST (Book #8)
ALREADY HIS (Book #9)
ALREADY LURED (Book #10)
ALREADY COLD (Book #11)

EUROPEAN VOYAGE COZY MYSTERY SERIES
MURDER (AND BAKLAVA) (Book #1)
DEATH (AND APPLE STRUDEL) (Book #2)
CRIME (AND LAGER) (Book #3)
MISFORTUNE (AND GOUDA) (Book #4)
CALAMITY (AND A DANISH) (Book #5)
MAYHEM (AND HERRING) (Book #6)

ADELE SHARP MYSTERY SERIES
LEFT TO DIE (Book #1)
LEFT TO RUN (Book #2)
LEFT TO HIDE (Book #3)
LEFT TO KILL (Book #4)
LEFT TO MURDER (Book #5)

LEFT TO ENVY (Book #6)
LEFT TO LAPSE (Book #7)
LEFT TO VANISH (Book #8)
LEFT TO HUNT (Book #9)
LEFT TO FEAR (Book #10)
LEFT TO PREY (Book #11)
LEFT TO LURE (Book #12)
LEFT TO CRAVE (Book #13)
LEFT TO LOATHE (Book #14)
LEFT TO HARM (Book #15)
LEFT TO RUIN (Book #16)

THE AU PAIR SERIES
ALMOST GONE (Book#1)
ALMOST LOST (Book #2)
ALMOST DEAD (Book #3)

ZOE PRIME MYSTERY SERIES
FACE OF DEATH (Book#1)
FACE OF MURDER (Book #2)
FACE OF FEAR (Book #3)
FACE OF MADNESS (Book #4)
FACE OF FURY (Book #5)
FACE OF DARKNESS (Book #6)

A JESSIE HUNT PSYCHOLOGICAL SUSPENSE SERIES
THE PERFECT WIFE (Book #1)
THE PERFECT BLOCK (Book #2)
THE PERFECT HOUSE (Book #3)
THE PERFECT SMILE (Book #4)
THE PERFECT LIE (Book #5)
THE PERFECT LOOK (Book #6)
THE PERFECT AFFAIR (Book #7)
THE PERFECT ALIBI (Book #8)
THE PERFECT NEIGHBOR (Book #9)
THE PERFECT DISGUISE (Book #10)
THE PERFECT SECRET (Book #11)
THE PERFECT FAÇADE (Book #12)
THE PERFECT IMPRESSION (Book #13)
THE PERFECT DECEIT (Book #14)
THE PERFECT MISTRESS (Book #15)

THE PERFECT IMAGE (Book #16)
THE PERFECT VEIL (Book #17)
THE PERFECT INDISCRETION (Book #18)
THE PERFECT RUMOR (Book #19)
THE PERFECT COUPLE (Book #20)
THE PERFECT MURDER (Book #21)
THE PERFECT HUSBAND (Book #22)
THE PERFECT SCANDAL (Book #23)
THE PERFECT MASK (Book #24)
THE PERFECT RUSE (Book #25)
THE PERFECT VENEER (Book #26)

CHLOE FINE PSYCHOLOGICAL SUSPENSE SERIES
NEXT DOOR (Book #1)
A NEIGHBOR'S LIE (Book #2)
CUL DE SAC (Book #3)
SILENT NEIGHBOR (Book #4)
HOMECOMING (Book #5)
TINTED WINDOWS (Book #6)

KATE WISE MYSTERY SERIES
IF SHE KNEW (Book #1)
IF SHE SAW (Book #2)
IF SHE RAN (Book #3)
IF SHE HID (Book #4)
IF SHE FLED (Book #5)
IF SHE FEARED (Book #6)
IF SHE HEARD (Book #7)

THE MAKING OF RILEY PAIGE SERIES
WATCHING (Book #1)
WAITING (Book #2)
LURING (Book #3)
TAKING (Book #4)
STALKING (Book #5)
KILLING (Book #6)

RILEY PAIGE MYSTERY SERIES
ONCE GONE (Book #1)
ONCE TAKEN (Book #2)
ONCE CRAVED (Book #3)

ONCE LURED (Book #4)
ONCE HUNTED (Book #5)
ONCE PINED (Book #6)
ONCE FORSAKEN (Book #7)
ONCE COLD (Book #8)
ONCE STALKED (Book #9)
ONCE LOST (Book #10)
ONCE BURIED (Book #11)
ONCE BOUND (Book #12)
ONCE TRAPPED (Book #13)
ONCE DORMANT (Book #14)
ONCE SHUNNED (Book #15)
ONCE MISSED (Book #16)
ONCE CHOSEN (Book #17)

MACKENZIE WHITE MYSTERY SERIES
BEFORE HE KILLS (Book #1)
BEFORE HE SEES (Book #2)
BEFORE HE COVETS (Book #3)
BEFORE HE TAKES (Book #4)
BEFORE HE NEEDS (Book #5)
BEFORE HE FEELS (Book #6)
BEFORE HE SINS (Book #7)
BEFORE HE HUNTS (Book #8)
BEFORE HE PREYS (Book #9)
BEFORE HE LONGS (Book #10)
BEFORE HE LAPSES (Book #11)
BEFORE HE ENVIES (Book #12)
BEFORE HE STALKS (Book #13)
BEFORE HE HARMS (Book #14)

AVERY BLACK MYSTERY SERIES
CAUSE TO KILL (Book #1)
CAUSE TO RUN (Book #2)
CAUSE TO HIDE (Book #3)
CAUSE TO FEAR (Book #4)
CAUSE TO SAVE (Book #5)
CAUSE TO DREAD (Book #6)

KERI LOCKE MYSTERY SERIES
A TRACE OF DEATH (Book #1)

A TRACE OF MURDER (Book #2)
A TRACE OF VICE (Book #3)
A TRACE OF CRIME (Book #4)
A TRACE OF HOPE (Book #5)

PROLOGUE

Cyndi Mayers sat up straight in bed, listening hard and feeling suddenly spooked. Was that a footstep she heard outside? Was someone slowly creeping up to her bedroom door so late in the night?

Nobody should be. She was the only occupant on this side of the corridor in this big, old house in rural Minnesota, where she and a few others were on a writers retreat.

It was a huge, creaky house, and the floorboards were noisy, which is what had clued her in and given her that shivery feeling. Even though she listened as hard as she could, she could hear nothing else.

Perhaps it had just been her imagination, she thought, letting out a breath and relaxing slightly. It could even be that her subconscious had invented the noise in order to help her with the opening lines of her horror novel.

She'd been struggling with it. She was hoping to come up with some creative ideas at this retreat. Cyndi wanted a spooky start to her horror story. Something that would grab the reader's attention and make them want to read on. Something that would make bookstore owners take notice. Something that would get her past the first three chapters, where her story always seemed to stick, before she lost faith in her plot and began again with a new idea.

She had so many concepts in her head, but the problem was that they didn't seem to translate to anything coherent on paper. She'd done so many exercises and group activities over the past few months. She'd been on three retreats. In her head, she could feel the start of the horror novel that would launch her into a brand-new career. But getting her thoughts into order on the page?

Impossible.

Cyndi sighed. She didn't think it was her fault any longer. Surely, it must be the fault of the retreat organizers. They'd promised to channel her talent into a constructive direction. They had guaranteed that she'd make progress with her writing.

She decided that she should probably ask for her money back because they were the ones who'd failed her. This retreat had cost a fortune. And she wasn't getting results, even though she'd been at it all day long. The accommodation, though atmospheric, wasn't five-star. Her bed squeaked, and the toilet flushed with a clank and a gurgle.

When she'd unpacked her things, she was sure she'd seen a spider scuttle into the dark corner of the closet.

And now that she'd had a look around the place, she wasn't sure she'd be able to write in her bedroom—or in the lounge or dining room. There were too many unexpected sounds. Too many distractions. She couldn't work with the wind howling.

She'd also been disappointed when she'd arrived and discovered that the others were mostly people like her. Ambitious but unpublished writers, looking to finish their works and hoping for that elusive break one day. There was nobody experienced to network with. Cyndi was great at networking. Her day job was sales. She knew that if she could network with the right person, she'd have a better chance of being published. A mentor could surely help her, but there were no mentors here.

She climbed out of bed, smoothed down her short dark hair, and walked over to the window, just to check, because she couldn't shake that uneasy feeling now that it had gotten into her head.

The wind was rattling the glass, as though it were trying to get in. She could see the lights of the small lakeside town in the distance. And behind her, on the shelf, the stone gargoyle stared blindly into space.

They'd tried, at least. They'd asked what she was writing, and she'd said horror, so they'd given her the Thrills and Chills room, on its own at the end of the corridor. The romance writer had the Boudoir, which overlooked the rather messy rose garden, and the others had rooms that they'd tried to decorate according to the writing themes.

But they hadn't tried hard enough. Cyndi pressed her lips together firmly. If they had tried harder, then she would be doing better after this first day.

With a sigh, she turned and picked up her notebook. She might as well write down how she felt now, and see if she could depict the spooky, uneasy feeling that she'd awoken with.

At least the weather was on her side, in terms of being chilling and atmospheric. The weather was playing its part on this blustery night.

Then Cyndi looked up from the page, turning her head. Over the wind, she heard a strange creaking noise. It seemed to be coming from somewhere outside her door. Was there someone around? Could an animal, or something, have wandered in here?

The only other room along the corridor was an old lounge, comfortable and historic, filled with old furniture and a few couches that had seen better days.

But now, Cyndi was starting to wonder about the door that led out of that lounge and into the large but unfenced grounds. She was wondering whether that door had been properly locked.

What if someone had broken in, she wondered. What if someone had come wandering inside, looking to help himself to the expensive laptops and electronics that the group had brought along?

That creaking hadn't been there a few minutes ago.

It would be better to go and see what it was, or at least to check that door. She didn't want to think of it standing open in the night. Her bedroom door locked, but only with a flimsy hook and eyelet on the inside of the door.

Now, Cyndi was getting seriously spooked. That's what came of writing horror all day. Now, she was imagining nightmare scenarios that went well beyond the normal.

Shivers cascaded down her spine as she thought about ghosts flitting through this old and dilapidated house, which had surely seen many deaths within its walls.

She opened her bedroom door and walked out into the corridor. The corridor was dark, despite the flickering light of the storm. The lights were flickering because of the wind, and she didn't trust the electrical connection to hold. Much more of this storm, she thought, and they'd be out of power.

She frowned as she saw the lounge door ahead. It was open. She knew it had been closed when she'd passed by earlier this evening.

Was it just the wind blowing it, or had someone opened this door recently? Now it was standing ajar, like a dark invitation to enter the lounge.

Cyndi felt her heart pounding, felt the unaccustomed and creepy sensation of adrenaline flooding into her veins. She let out a slow breath as she pushed the door, and it swung all the way open with a creak.

Were there any lights in here? Along the wall, perhaps?

She felt her way, but at that moment, in a violent gust of wind, the corridor light blinked out.

She gasped. She was standing in total darkness, and she felt a strange and terrifying moment of disorientation. Then anger prevailed. This place was a dump! They couldn't even get the electronics to work correctly. What hope did she have for finishing her book? This retreat was unbelievable, she thought furiously.

Then a lightning flash showed her where the window was. Now that her eyes were used to the dark, she saw it was slightly lighter there. A faint glow, from a mostly hidden three-quarter moon. It lit up the stacks of furniture: that hulking couch, the weird old rolltop desk, and the bookshelves with piles of dusty volumes.

The outside door. Was it open? It looked open, and her heart sped up again as another lightning flash gave her a tantalizing glimpse.

If it was open, she needed to close it and fast. And then, she needed to call the organizers in case an intruder had gotten in.

Those floorboards creaking had sounded like someone walking. Like slow, regular footsteps.

Shivers prickled her arms again as she moved forward, picking her way and waiting for the surges of lightning, which were fast and frequent now.

But as she moved, Cyndi began to have the horrible feeling that she was not alone. She felt sure that there was someone else in this room—a hidden, undetectable presence. She might have been imagining it, but it felt like she was being watched by a malevolent presence.

Maybe she was just being foolish. The setting and the storm were making her imagination run rampant. It was making her think that there was something here.

A gust of wind, louder than ever before, screamed through the window, letting in a blast of cold rain.

She reached the door. It wasn't open but was, in fact, closed. Testing it, she turned the handle.

It was locked.

"Well," Cyndi muttered to herself, feeling ever so slightly deflated from her righteous anger. It was locked, so nobody could have gotten in. All her feelings had been wrong. At least nobody had come this way. That was the main thing, especially since her instincts weren't listening to common sense. Her heart was still racing, even though her thoughts were calmer.

She turned back the way she'd come, waiting for the next lightning flash to show her the way to the corridor.

It came, and the eerie, cool light illuminated the room. The furniture.

And it illuminated a shape in front of her, a shape literally rising from the floor.

A dark, threatening shadow of a being that was as impossible as it was real. She'd just landed in a scenario more frightening, more horrific, than she'd ever imagined in the pages of her future bestseller.

"No!" Cyndi screamed.

There was someone here. A ghost, a specter, a terrible and evil being that was now making its way to her, hands outstretched. She saw bony fingers, lit up by the next lightning flash, clutching a weapon that looked big, solid, and heavy, raised high above its head. The face beyond was shrouded in darkness.

"Please, no! Help!" Cyndi screamed.

She turned and ran, but in her panic, plowed into one of the wooden tables and went sprawling.

"Help!" she screamed again, now hysterical with fear.

She tried to scream once more, but abruptly, the world flickered into darkness.

CHAPTER ONE

"Hey, Kerry!" Sitting at her kitchen table, Deputy May Moore felt glad that her FBI agent sister had picked up her early morning call. There was a lot to discuss, and she felt a sense of urgency about all of it.

She'd recently discovered more information on their sister's missing persons case. The evidence, hidden away in a safe unopened for years, suggested that Lauren was one of a number of victims taken—by someone—around ten years ago, or perhaps longer.

Her pink baseball cap had been found in the safe, along with other items that May thought belonged to other young women.

May had examined and logged each of the items and was now trying to compare them to other cold cases, looking at the time frame of when Lauren had disappeared. There was no doubt these items had been hidden away in the safe for more than seven years.

Meanwhile, Kerry was analyzing the footage of the threat video that May had found on her laptop a while ago when she'd gotten back from work.

Someone had left footage of Lauren, marching angrily out of the house on the day she'd been taken. The video had warned May to back off.

Now, she and Kerry were working together on this case. With the evidence, and the video, May was sure they had enough to lead them to this criminal.

Her kitchen window overlooked farm fields in the small town of Fairshore, Tamarack County, Minnesota. But at seven a.m. on an early fall morning, the curtains were closed, and the window was still gloomy. Clouds from a late-night rainstorm were beginning to clear. A cup of coffee steamed by her laptop as she went through her latest research with her sister.

"Have you looked at the footage?" May asked, putting her phone on speaker while she scooped her sandy-blond hair back into a ponytail.

"I have," Kerry said.

"And? Is there any way of finding out more?"

"There is. There's something in the footage that I can use, sis," Kerry told her, her voice ringing with confidence.

"What's that?" May asked, feeling hopeful.

"It's a dead pixel."

"That little black dot near the right-hand corner?" May asked.

"Yup. Now, that would be from a camera defect. The camera would probably have had that error consistently."

"Okay?" May asked. She felt excited by that. Consistency was always good, right? It improved the chances of something being traced back.

"There's other footage from this area available from that time. It's online, it's stored, and it's on social media. And we're going through what there is. I have one of the best techs helping me in his spare time. We're searching for that same issue, looking for any other footage that might have been taken from that camera and ended up published."

"That's brilliant," May said. She paused. "You think you'll actually pick something up though? I mean, it's a lot of footage."

"Are you saying I can't do it?" Kerry snapped back.

May sighed. Sisterly bickering was not going to help them here. The bright, ambitious Kerry was always super defensive when you dared to doubt her ability. And she'd been especially on edge since her wedding was called off after she'd discovered her fiancé was cheating. Kerry didn't like it when things went wrong in her life. She was a perfectionist. And now, May sensed she was trying to prove herself all over again after that personal catastrophe.

"I'm just asking, is all," May said. "I'm on your side here. No disrespect intended. But, you know, it's hundreds of thousands of videos, surely?"

"Not so much, ten years ago," Kerry said. "Not from this county. There wasn't nearly as much as there is today. So, it's going to be doable. It just has to be done!" She sounded determined.

I'm sure you'll find what you're looking for," May said, hoping she sounded more confident than she felt.

"And your side? Any items from other cases matching up with what you found in the safe?" Kerry asked.

"No. Nothing concrete yet. But at least I've now gotten all the missing persons cases listed, from seven to fifteen years ago, that are still cold. All the cases in the county and beyond. I don't know how far afield this man might have gone."

"And?"

"And there are quite a few cases that might be relevant. I'm looking for women in particular, as the items in that safe all seemed to belong to women."

"That makes sense. Slow work I guess," Kerry said.

May didn't miss the tone in her voice that told her Kerry was sure she could do it faster.

"I have to have everything listed," May continued defensively. "If someone was taking these women, and didn't get caught for ten years, it means he or she was very careful, thorough. So, I have to be the same way."

"Yes, yes, I know. I guess in a local police department, you don't really have the technology or manpower to help you."

"No, I don't!" Now May was mad. How did Kerry always manage to get her feeling that way? She felt as if that snide remark was not just comparing their circumstances unfavorably, but their entire lives.

"I'm doing what I can, okay?" she snapped to Kerry. "And I'm the one who found the safe! I'm the one who's found everything so far! Made all the breakthroughs!"

Seething, she sprang to her feet. Staring angrily at her coffee cup, she drained the contents in one annoyed gulp.

But strangely, now that she realized her sister was mad, Kerry wasn't pushing it. In fact, to her surprise, May realized she was backing off on the baiting.

"I know," Kerry said, her tone less accusatory now. "You're doing the right thing. It's frustrating work on both ends. I wish this could be solved, now."

"I feel the same way," May said, sitting down again, calmer now. "Maybe we just need some luck, some inspiration. Some great leap in technology. I don't know."

Ten years of not knowing was long enough. Ten years of nightmares and memories—of missing her sister and wondering whether she was still alive.

She guessed, though, that in context, a few weeks of research was nothing compared to the time that had already passed, and that was what she needed to keep telling herself. If she got too discouraged by the slow pace, she'd never get anywhere.

Plus, she couldn't allow herself to get distracted from her duties as deputy. Her day job had to come first. May knew that the safety of her community took priority. Imagine if she neglected her job, and as a result, someone else ended up suffering terrible consequences? May would never be able to live with herself if that happened.

"I'm going to keep looking through the old cases," May said.

"And I'll keep going through the footage," Kerry said. "I've got to go now. Gotta get to work. Busy day."

"I'll call you if I find anything," May said.

"Me too."

They cut the call, but it began ringing again, and she saw this time it was her boss on the line.

Quickly, she grabbed it, knowing that an early call like this would be important and that it might mean a serious crime.

"Morning, Sheriff Jack," she said.

"Morning, May," Jack said. He sounded stressed. "We have an urgent situation here. We've had two murders occur in the small town of Cole Hill within a day of each other, in neighboring properties in the historic area. They've literally both been called in, first thing this morning."

May felt her heart clench. Multiple murders? Two victims on two properties? Were they connected in any way? What were the circumstances?

What was going on in that sleepy, historic town? How had such a thing happened?

Already she had a multitude of questions, and she knew she wouldn't be the only one asking them. There would be widespread panic surging in the place that was one of the area's fastest growing tourist destinations. May knew she had to get there fast. This was a disaster in the making.

"Please send the coordinates. I'm on my way right now," she said, grabbing her bag and heading for the door.

CHAPTER TWO

What was going on in Cole Hill? May fretted, hitting the gas as she sped along the winding road that led to the scenic town. It sounded as if someone had gone on a killing spree. In Cole Hill, of all places?

It was one of the quietest towns in Tamarack County, tucked away between rolling hills, bordering a small tributary of the lake, with river frontage, and also one of the area's oldest towns, with many historic buildings.

The new town mayor had been campaigning for the past two years, promoting the town, bringing in new tourism opportunities, and creating a thriving industry, which had so far been very successful.

Now this had happened, and it was nothing short of a disaster. May clenched the wheel as she drove into Cole Hill, noting the new "Welcome" board that had been installed at the town's entrance, the fresh blacktop on the road, and the well-tended flower beds that surrounded the signage.

The Cole Hill community had done so much to spruce up the place. But nobody wanted to visit a place where murders had occurred. These deaths would mean a huge setback to the town's lively progress. She knew Cole Hill's long-term reputation was at risk if this didn't get sorted quickly.

May checked the coordinates that Jack had sent her.

It seemed the murders had been reported from Windrush Road, which May thought was the prettiest road in the whole town—close to the lake and lined with old historic houses, many of which were in the process of being renovated. Tall maple trees graced the road, which wound its way down to a cul-de-sac in a beautiful park by the river.

"Two murders," May said aloud, slowing down as she pulled up to the yellow police cordon.

Already there were a few police cars there, along with an ambulance and a coroner's van. And Owen's car. May was pleased to see her investigation partner, and budding romantic interest, was already there. At least this was one good thing in what was sure to be a very difficult morning. The tall, dark-haired Owen looked stressed, but his expression softened as he saw her arrive. Having clearly been on the scene a few minutes with Sheriff Jack, he rushed over.

"There are two bodies, one in each of the houses," he said. "It looks as if one woman was killed the night before last, and one woman last night, but they were both only found this morning. There's no sign of forced entry visible."

"And the cause of death?" May asked, already feeling her blood pressure skyrocket.

"It looks to be the same in both instances. Andy Baker is here, working on the earlier of the two kills, so he can tell you more."

Thank goodness Andy was already on the scene because May needed answers. She stared at the two gracious historic homes, with their arched windows and pillared porches. What could have happened within these freshly painted walls?

May saw, glancing down the road, that shocked people were filing out of the front door of the home where the second murder had occurred. A woman in a green jacket was arranging seating for them under the trees on the lawn, clearly wanting them to be somewhere out of the way while the police did their work.

Feeling her heart beat faster, May hurried to the first scene, stepping under the crime scene tape and quickly pulling on her protective foot covers and gloves before entering.

There was Andy. She saw him ahead, in the corridor leading to the stairs, near a room to the right.

Andy glanced up, his face serious. "Morning, May. We've most definitely got the same killer in both circumstances here."

"What was the cause of death?" May asked. Andy was bent over the corpse, so all May could see was that the woman looked to be wearing a dressing gown and fluffy slippers.

"Both of these victims seem to have been attacked with a weapon made from wood, and it seems as if both attacks occurred at night. I'm not sure what it was with, but both victims were hit over the head. A hard, fatal blow. There are visible splinters of white-painted wood in this wound."

"So, this victim would have been killed the night before last then?" May asked.

"Yes. She's been dead probably thirty hours. She was staying here alone. Her name is Marie Everton according to her ID, and the police just told me she was an event organizer, from out of town, preparing for a team building event that was happening in the house. Setting up the sound systems, the music, the audio visuals. When she was uncontactable, her colleague from the company arrived early this morning and found her dead. He took one look and called the police. So, the scene is undisturbed."

"Did he give any other information?" May asked.

"He said, when he reported the crime, that there was no way Marie would have gone to bed without locking up. So, I guess there's a chance the killer might have come in earlier and hidden away, and then let himself out when he was done."

"Where is the colleague?" Owen asked.

"He drove straight back home. He was very shaken. I arrived as he was leaving. He didn't want to stay in the area, he said."

May nodded. His reaction was understandable. And if this woman had been killed the night before last, it was unlikely her colleague would have seen or heard anything helpful.

Instead, May took a closer look at the scene herself.

The nearby room was a bedroom, she saw. It had a four-poster bed, an old-fashioned wardrobe, and a big bookshelf. May felt a frisson of dread as she imagined what must have played out. Had the woman heard the killer outside her room and come out to see what was happening?

May guessed that having the occupant of the house busily preparing for an event, bringing equipment in and setting it up, would have allowed the killer enough time to sneak in and hide.

"And the other victim? What was she doing in that nearby home?"

"That was the venue for a writers retreat. The other guests are still there. I'm not sure of that victim's name yet, but her body was found this morning, when one of the retreat guests went into the lounge. I've only glanced at that body, but the cause of death is definitely the same."

May glanced around this house, where the first kill had taken place. It was clearly old, and although in the process of being well renovated, it still looked tumbledown in a few places. She guessed that in a team building event, that atmosphere might provide a fun environment.

"I wonder if there's any evidence he might have left behind," May said. "It might be worth taking a look through the houses. This is where he made the first kill. Perhaps he left something behind, or we could find a footprint?" May suggested to Owen. "Once we've done that, we could head across to the other house and speak to the witnesses there."

"Let's get started," Owen agreed.

As she walked farther into the home, which smelled of fresh paint and wood polish, Owen asked her in a low voice, "Is everything okay, May?"

She turned, looking at the dark-haired deputy, feeling surprised by the question. And at the same time, she felt a flash of guilt, because she hadn't told him everything that had happened recently in her hunt for answers with Lauren's case.

It had felt too personal, like too much info. May hadn't wanted to dump such a massive, complex issue into the lap of someone who was a new love interest in her life. Owen didn't deserve to have to listen to every development in what May was recognizing was something that she was slightly obsessed with. She was trying to keep this separate from her budding romance.

So, she shook her head. "No, everything's fine," she replied, feeling bad to be glossing over the facts, but deciding that the time to tell him would be when she had more answers to give.

It didn't seem fair to be telling Owen all this stuff before she was even sure of what she was going to do, or what would happen next.

"Okay, then. Let's get to work," he said. But May could tell he wasn't convinced. Owen was too smart and too perceptive to believe nothing was wrong. The silence between them felt slightly uneasy.

Then May turned away, deciding that the best way to cope with this would be to get back to work. They had an important job to do here, looking for evidence that the killer might have left behind.

They started out in the old kitchen, with a massive gas stove, a huge wooden counter, and antique cupboards that had been sanded and varnished to a glossy shine.

The kitchen was clearly in use. Food had been placed in the new fridge in the corner, ready for the event ahead. Coffee and tea were on the counter. The place looked clean and was free from dust.

"I don't think we're going to find anything here," May said doubtfully. The killer clearly hadn't hidden out here, as she couldn't see any signs that he might have been here.

They walked out of the kitchen, stepping carefully in their protective foot covers, and May headed along the corridor to the lounge.

This room, too, looked to have been recently cleaned, and May couldn't see any signs or evidence that the killer might have hidden here. A large sound system with speakers had been set up, and there was a small stack of additional chairs that she guessed Marie was going to set out. Beyond the kitchen, she saw a utility room that was empty and dark, and there was a space where she guessed a washing machine should be. There was a crumpled tarp there. Perhaps he'd hidden under it, pulled it over himself, and waited there? That was a possibility, and forensics could check the area for trace evidence, but for now there was nothing else to see down here.

It would be worthwhile looking upstairs.

But, as they were heading up the winding wooden staircase, tramping on the worn but polished treads, Owen grabbed her arm.

May jumped. There was something about this old house that was making her feel very spooked, and the sudden touch had startled her.

"What is it?" she asked.

Owen was pointing up the stairs, to the top of the staircase.

"There, May. Look there. That might be important!"

May looked. Her eyes widened.

When she saw where he was pointing, and what it might mean, her blood ran cold.

She hurried up the stairs, to look more closely at what might be their first critical piece of evidence.

CHAPTER THREE

May rushed up the stairs, wondering if she was following the exact route the killer had taken. She thought she might be doing just that, because, at the top of the stairs, one of the white, wooden balustrade rails was broken cleanly away, leaving only a jagged piece of wood at the bottom.

She and Owen stared down at the missing piece.

"This was deliberately broken, for sure. I mean, the rest of the staircase is in good condition. Solid. It's not falling apart," May said.

"And Andy picked up white splinters in the wound," Owen agreed. "If he had broken in and then decided to kill, maybe he just grabbed the first weapon he could see."

"And this was the house where the first victim was found," May said. "I wonder if it was preplanned, or if he was thinking on the fly. He broke in, saw the victim, and decided then and there to kill?"

Grabbing a weapon on site, at the time, meant they were dealing with an impulsive, irrational killer rather than a cold-minded preplanner. That would be important in profiling him, May decided.

At any rate, she thought they'd more than likely discovered what the weapon was. Now, they would need to get the forensic team in here and dust for fingerprints. She was shocked by the brutality it would have taken to rip this piece of wood out and use it to hit someone over the head. They were dealing with someone violent and, May thought, unhinged.

However, looking at the top floor of the house, May could see a faint sheen of dust across the wooden floorboards. The stairs had been dusted, but not the area beyond. And there were no footprints to be seen. So, without a doubt, since the dust was not disturbed, the killer had only been far enough up the stairs to grab his weapon and wrench it from out of the wooden stairway. Nobody else had been any farther, not even Marie. She must have been planning to prepare the upper floor today, May thought sadly.

"I guess we need to go and talk to the people next door," Owen said. May saw he was also looking keenly at the dust.

"Let's speak to them," May said, feeling frustrated that this scene hadn't yielded more.

They left the house, ducked under the crime scene tape, and headed to the next-door home where all the occupants of the house were seated under the trees. May felt that they would be ready to talk, since the shock of the death had now had a few minutes to sink in, and they were all talking nonstop to each other.

She quickly detoured to the police officer who was stringing crime scene tape up at the door.

"Do we have an ID for the victim?" she asked, wanting to know this information before she approached the witnesses.

"Yes, she's Cyndi Mayers from Massachusetts, aged forty-five."

"Thank you," May said.

Armed with this information, she approached the small group, giving a sympathetic nod of welcome. She could imagine how traumatizing this must have been, to have been on a writers retreat and have such a thing happen.

There were three women sitting on a bench. The blond woman was about twenty-five, the brunette looked to be in her forties, and the gray-haired woman was probably sixty years of age.

On the next-door bench, two men who both looked fifty-plus years of age, were deep in discussion.

They were both looking very serious, sipping on their coffee, and the older one had a notebook open on the table in front of him with a pen poised.

"Tragic as this is, every experience must go into the writer's artillery of material," she heard him say, before he began scribbling furiously. "From great shock and grief, stories are born."

May approached the group.

"Look, the police are here!" the older woman said breathlessly.

"I'm sorry we have to be here in such shocking circumstances, but we need to ask you folks a few questions," May said.

The women all exchanged glances, and now the men looked up curiously, too.

"Of course," the blond said. "We'll be glad to help. This has been so traumatic."

"Did you know the victim, Cyndi Mayers, at all? When did you meet her?"

They all looked at each other again.

"We only met her when we arrived here yesterday morning. We were all strangers until then," the brunette explained.

"She was a lovely person. This is so awful," the blond woman said, putting an arm around the shoulder of the woman next to her.

"Her death is a tragedy. I can't believe it. And now the retreat is canceled and we're all trying to change our flights to go home again. Jeanie, the poor organizer, is busy with it now in town. And she's the one who found the body! She should be lying down now, getting over the shock, not rushing around to help us."

"Since you have been here, did you notice anything out of the ordinary happening? Anyone watching the place, any attempted crimes, any incidents at all?" May asked.

All the writers looked thoughtful.

"Well, it was quite a spooky house. Atmospheric," the older man said.

"I heard noises last night, for sure," the blonde added. "I thought it was haunted."

"And the house itself is so magnificent but so run down. There are so many rooms, and so many of them seem unused," the gray-haired woman admitted.

"Were any of the doors left unlocked?" May asked.

The blonde shrugged. "Yes. I think Jeanie locked up last thing at night, but none of us thought it was dangerous here. I walked out into the garden through the kitchen door after dark, to look at the moon. It felt eerie, but none of us dreamed there was a killer nearby."

"Did any of you hear anything last night?" May asked.

"It did feel as though there was something else here, from the time I arrived," the brunette said. "I felt as though I was being watched."

"We all felt that," the older woman said. "But we assumed it was just part of the atmosphere."

"Cyndi also picked that up. In fact, she was probably the one out of all of us who complained the most. Yesterday evening, she said her room was noisy, and she wasn't able to focus properly," the blond remembered. "Maybe she sensed something, now I think about it."

May thought this was interesting because instincts were often a big sign that something was wrong. Clearly all the writers had instinctively felt that there was someone else around.

"They said the house has an old basement with a hidden entrance," the brunette said. "I remember reading somewhere else also about a secret room. That must be the basement, right?"

"The secret room wasn't listed in the description of the house. But Jeanie told me on the way here when she fetched me from the airport," the blonde said. "I was looking forward to hunting for it yesterday but ended up being too busy with my scene where the heroine first meets the hero. You know, it's such a delicate yet pivotal moment and I simply couldn't get it right."

"I understand," Owen sympathized.

"So, I was working on that, drawing energy from these peaceful surroundings, and didn't get time to explore and search. Plus, I'm a romance writer, so finding a hidden room wouldn't really have furthered my plot in any way."

"As a thriller writer, I intended to look for it," the brunette said firmly. "But I was battling with my scene where the villain stalks his first victim. Stupid logistics, you know how it is?"

"Exactly," the other writers said.

"So just because I couldn't work out how to get him hidden away in plain sight, I never looked for it either!" She sighed impatiently.

May glanced at Owen.

She didn't think that there was anything further to be gained from these interviews, as everyone had recently met, and there had been no obvious problems.

But she was interested to know more about that basement.

"Thank you so much. You've been really helpful. Good luck with your writing, and I hope that you are able to put this horrible experience behind you soon," she sympathized.

She moved a few steps away with Owen.

"This basement," she said.

"Yes, I think we should find it, May. It might be the killer's hiding place. Perhaps he's been using it as a hideout while he stalked these victims, or else he waited down there and we might find evidence inside."

May wasn't going to allow herself to get too optimistic, but she couldn't help a flare of excitement that there had been a secret hiding place. Looking at the house, you could actually see it. There was a lower area where the building sloped down, and she saw tiny ventilation grids in a few of the bricks close to floor level, which were guarded by an overhang that must have been placed there for a reason.

"Now, to see if we can find it," she said. "Shall we start by looking in the house?"

May headed to the spooky house where the most recent murder had taken place, hoping that the killer had left some signs of his presence, or identity, hidden away.

CHAPTER FOUR

May walked tentatively into the house where the murder had occurred, with Owen close behind. This was all so recent that the corpse was still in place. Andy hadn't had a chance to do the preliminary examination yet. Her spine was prickling, and she felt uneasy in these creepy surroundings.

And they were creepy. This house hadn't been renovated as thoroughly as the one next door and was still very dark and old fashioned. They both walked slowly through the house, looking for a basement entrance or a stairway going down.

Heading into the lounge, May saw the walls were lined with wood paneling, and the furniture was heavy and dark.

There were thick curtains at the windows, and May imagined she could almost hear the ghostly voices that must have echoed down these corridors for centuries.

There was a fireplace that looked to be in use and still had traces of a fire. There were several armchairs upholstered in wine-red fabric that looked faded, and a scuffed side table with an evil-looking metal candlestick holder.

And there was the body. She caught her breath as she saw the flash of turquoise from the woman's nightdress. She was lying sprawled near an overturned chair.

"I guess there was a struggle of some kind, or she tried to escape?" May breathed. She paced closer, steeling herself as she looked down. This body had not yet been closely examined so she didn't want to contaminate the scene but wanted to check that it was without a doubt the same manner of death.

It was. She bit her lip as she saw the distinct head wound. She could actually see what looked like a white splinter in the victim's hair. It was the same MO, and she was sure Andy Baker would confirm it when he examined the corpse. So, the killer had kept his strange, unusual weapon that had been wrenched from the neighboring house's staircase and was now using it again. That was weird! Was there a reason why he was using something from the home itself, to kill? Did it have significance to him?

Goose bumps chilled her arms. It felt incredibly spooky in here. She could see exactly why the other writers had picked up on the uneasy ambiance.

Even without a corpse, this room was creepy. But they were not here to pay close attention to the body and May didn't want to disturb the scene in any way. Andy Baker's expertise would hopefully draw those secrets out.

For now, they needed to figure out where the basement was.

Glancing at the floor, May saw to her disappointment that the wooden boards were clean, free from dust, and no footprints were visible.

"Could the basement be down here?" Owen asked, moving to the side of the room where there was a railing.

They walked over and May immediately saw it wasn't going to be so easy. The railing seemed to lead nowhere. It was as if an entrance point might have existed sometime in the past but had long since been boarded over.

"We need to look somewhere else," she decided.

Together they left the lounge and moved along the corridor. There were bedrooms on either side, and then beyond, May saw a darkened room that looked to be a dining room.

That sparked her interest. Perhaps a dining room might lead down to the basement, if the owners of the home had stored wine or food in a cooler, underground place.

"Shall we look in here?" she asked.

The dining room was impressive, with a long table and chairs, and another huge fireplace that dominated one wall, and a massive wine rack on another.

It was dark, and the overhead chandelier cast only a dim glow, so May had to take her phone out and activate the flashlight in order to see the floor clearly, as she didn't want to risk obliterating any evidence. The windows were covered in thick blinds. Perhaps they could be raised, but she didn't want to do it in case they broke. That was the feeling she had with this house, that it was so old it had developed its own personality.

May had a thought. With the house being so old, would a fireplace have enough space to be a hidden entrance to the basement?

"Owen, could this fireplace be the basement entrance? It's big enough for a person to climb down," she suggested. "It doesn't look to have been recently used. And perhaps the chimney shaft provided access to an otherwise unused room?"

He considered it, and then gave a shrug.

"It's possible. Shall we see?"

They paced to the fireplace, which May estimated was definitely in the correct place to be near the basement.

She shone her flashlight in and caught her breath.

She'd never thought she'd be right. It had honestly just been a guess. But now, she could see that a dark gap in the back of the fireplace led to a steep and very rusted looking staircase. It plummeted down into darkness, making all of May's nerves start tingling.

"This is weird," she said, feeling suddenly doubtful.

"Let's head down for a look-see," Owen suggested.

If he wasn't scared, then she could be brave too. May inched into the stairwell, gasping as her feet touched the clanging rails. It was cold and very silent. She couldn't shake the feeling that something was reaching out to grasp her ankles. In fact, she couldn't quite bear to look down and see how far the drop was. Most probably, in the darkness, she wouldn't be able to see anyway.

With a flash of fear, she shined her flashlight around, illuminating old and peeling walls. But at least the place looked empty. There didn't seem to be anyone hiding there.

As they made their way down the metal steps, May couldn't help but wonder if they were going to make a huge discovery. Was this going to be the breakthrough they needed?

She clutched onto the slippery, rusting sides of the staircase rail as she clambered down. And then finally, she reached the bottom. She didn't want to move any farther or make any marks that might obliterate the traces that someone else had been there, so she stood on her tiptoes, as still as possible, clutching the ladder with one hand and reaching for her flashlight with the other.

The air here smelled cold and stale. May shined her flashlight around, looking for any hiding places where someone might be lurking, or any sign that somebody was hiding out here.

But it looked very exposed. There were no hiding places, no means by which somebody could have sneaked up on them.

She could see a doorway in the wall, where an area had been bricked up, and she could see a few old pieces of furniture, some of which seemed to have been draped in dust sheets.

Owen's flashlight joined hers, increasing the amount of light available.

But, to May's disappointment, the dust here looked to be undisturbed. She couldn't see the faintest trace of any footprints. The killer hadn't been down here. Nobody had been down here. It was a brilliant secret room, but it hadn't been used as a hideout.

So, May found herself thinking that the writers' instincts might have been wrong. This killer might not have been hiding in the house. The noises they heard could just have been the creaks and groans of an old house settling, made worse by the breezy day. Perhaps he'd arrived late at night, sneaked inside, and just taken temporary cover in a bathroom or in the lounge itself, where Cyndi had unfortunately walked in and been the first to meet him.

"Should we go up now?" May suggested, glancing at the time on her phone. "Jeanie, the organizer, might be back by now. And she's someone we need to speak to. If anyone knows more details that the guests haven't yet been told, it's her."

CHAPTER FIVE

May felt relieved to climb up that shaky steel ladder and out of the basement. It had been a creepy experience that had seemed to be so promising, but it had ultimately resulted in a dead end. There was still no evidence or sign of this killer. He was totally anonymous.

They now needed to move fast in catching up with him, and she hoped that the retreat organizer would have more information.

May and Owen hurried out of the house, to find Sheriff Jack and Andy Baker approaching. Quickly, May briefed her boss on their progress so far.

"We need forensics to examine the utility room next door, which has an old tarp lying in it. It's the only place that we think he might have been able to hide and wait. There's an old basement here, but it has layers of dust on the floor that are definitely undisturbed. And at the top of the staircase, a balustrade was broken off. It looks like that was used as the murder weapon, so perhaps there are fingerprints on the rail."

Jack nodded. "We'll get forensics to work in the other house as soon as they can get here. I'm going to get on the phone to them now and tell them what they need to check. But they'll probably only be able to make a start tomorrow." He headed quickly toward the other house.

May knew from experience that even in the most urgent local crimes, the forensic team often had a backlog. Their local forensic unit was just one expert team, servicing a large area. Delays were inevitable and once again, May felt a flash of envy for Kerry, who was able to summon up seemingly limitless FBI resources within mere minutes of a crime taking place.

What a difference it made. Sometimes, she felt her hands were tied by the slowness with which operations took place in Tamarack County. But May knew this meant that she, as the local deputy, needed to focus even more on the crimes. Where forensics was slow, deduction and attention to detail could fill in the gaps.

As May walked out of the house, a smart, sleek black car pulled up outside. Hoping this was Jeanie, she hurried over to it.

But, as the door opened and the occupant of the car climbed out, she realized to her dismay that this was not Jeanie.

The man scrambling purposefully out of this sleek vehicle was short and sturdy, had receding brown hair, and was wearing a stylish suit that made the most of his rather square build.

May recognized him immediately.

This was Mayor Tillman, the new driving force behind Cole Hill, and the one who'd been promoting tourism in town, leading to so many positive changes.

Even though May knew that Mayor Tillman worked tirelessly, and while she respected his vision for the town, she didn't like him personally, having met him in a town meeting once. He was rude and abrupt to anyone who wasn't actually involved in helping him, and he didn't seem to like the police at all.

This impression was reinforced when he focused on her and Owen with a laser-like gaze and glared at them.

"What the hell is going on here? This kind of crime should not be happening in this town!" he shouted.

Not even so much as a good morning. This man was seriously upset. And May couldn't blame him. The gruesome deaths of two tourists were going to be headline news. They would put Cole Hill in the spotlight for all the wrong reasons. Having these tragic deaths would keep tourists away, starving the town of the lifeblood it needed.

"We're so sorry, Mayor Tillman," May said respectfully. "It's an absolute tragedy and we're going to be working around the clock to arrest this killer."

She hoped her words were reassuring, but Mayor Tillman didn't seem in the least reassured.

"You mean you've arrested nobody yet?" Clearly unimpressed with the promise of their efforts ahead, Tillman glowered deeper. "I don't want you working around the clock. I need results sooner than that. I am going to be on a panel with potential investors this afternoon," he said. "I need more answers, immediately. This is a disaster. A disaster!" he said, pacing up and down.

The man was clearly distressed, and May felt for him. She understood the pressure he was under. She just wished that he could be more understanding of the fact that the police had not caused these murders, would have been unable to prevent such a crime, and needed more than a few minutes to solve such a complex case, with a killer who'd seemingly materialized out of thin air and then disappeared again.

Tillman didn't look ready to accommodate any delays, and May had a sinking feeling that his interference and pressuring was only going to create problems. There was absolutely no point in telling him that though. It would only make him madder.

"As I said, we're working as hard as we can," May said, hoping this would at least calm him down.

"You need to work harder," he said. "I mean, you're public servants, right? Our tax money pays your wages!"

"We are going to do whatever we can to get this solved. We rushed here as soon as the crimes were called in, and we're going to be doing nothing else until they're solved. We're going to leave no stone unturned. We're not going to sleep until a killer is arrested, and we'll hopefully make progress by tonight." May promised, aware she was resorting to clichés and making promises she might not be able to keep. But she felt desperate to calm him down and convince him that the police were not totally incompetent.

"I need this to be over and done with and fast. We've just spent literally hundreds of thousands on uplifting and promoting this town. And now we have police, dragging their feet and refusing to solve a serious crime in a hurry."

May resented his implication that all the police were capable of was eating doughnuts and lazily watching the clock. Clearly, Mayor Tillman was now resorting to personal insults in an effort to speed things up.

Already, having to placate him was wasting time, especially since May had just seen another car pull up.

A stressed looking woman with wild brunette hair was scrambling out, and she felt sure this was Jeanie. She needed to be speaking to her, not getting berated by the mayor.

May could see Jeanie regarding the two of them in a questioning way. She was moving a step closer to them and then hesitating. From her demeanor, May guessed it meant she had something to say.

Twisting her fingers, Jeanie waited a moment, and then as someone called her name, she turned and walked back to the writers, as frustration flared inside May.

"We're doing all that we can," May said neutrally to the mayor. "And if you'll excuse us, we have to go and interview a witness who's just arrived."

This didn't seem to encourage Tillman in the slightest. He stared from May to Owen and back again, seeming to like nothing he saw whatsoever.

"I just want you to be aware that I'm watching you," Tillman said. "I'm monitoring what you are doing, and how you are investigating. There will be an official report. I'm going to request one. I'm going to come to your police department tomorrow, and go through your affairs with a fine toothcomb, looking for any signs of incompetence. If I find any, there'll be hell to pay. You need to know that, Deputy, and tell your boss. I've gone head-to-head with the sheriff in the past, and I won't hesitate to take drastic steps. And rest assured, the steps I take will not be good for your careers. Not for any of you!"

Then he turned on his heel and stormed back to his car. With a shriek of tires, he accelerated away.

May and Owen watched him go, then Owen shook his head. "I'm worried, May. This mayor seems to have serious issues with us. How can he say such things? Do you think he means them?"

"He cares a lot about this town," May said, trying to be reasonable rather than critical. "He cares very much. And he's under a lot of pressure. But he doesn't understand how difficult it is to investigate a murder."

"No, he doesn't. And his threats were worrying."

"I'm sure he's not going to try to get any of us fired," May said, wishing she believed her own words more strongly.

"He's not a nice man, is he?" Owen said, shaking his head.

"He's furious," May said. "He's worried about the damage to tourism, and rightly so. I don't blame him for being mad. I just wish he'd been a bit more understanding about the fact that we're all doing our best."

"Well, we'd better get on with the investigation," Owen agreed.

May nodded. "Let's go and speak to Jeanie. I noticed she was trying to approach us earlier, but she didn't want to interrupt the mayor. It looked like she might have information. We can get it from her now. If we're lucky, it might mean we finally have a lead."

CHAPTER SIX

May hurried over to Jeanie, the writers retreat organizer, hearing the revving of the car's engine as the angry mayor departed. This pressure from him was complicating the case and adding a new sense of urgency.

She needed results and hoped that the stressed-looking Jeanie could provide them.

"I'm deputy Moore and this is deputy Lovell," she introduced herself and Owen. "We're so sorry this has happened."

Jeanie turned to her with tears in her reddened blue eyes. "I can't believe it. It's a nightmare come true. We're all so traumatized. I've just been on a call with Cyndi's brother, trying to give him some answers. I told him she was enjoying herself. Everyone was having a good time, and then this happened. It's just so unthinkable. And yet, now I look back, I think there were signs something was wrong."

"Tell me about the retreat. Are you the organizer? Are you from this town yourself?" May asked, wanting some background before she asked more about the signs Jeanie had mentioned.

"I'm the retreat organizer, yes. I handle the guest list and all the logistics. Everything from booking the venue to arranging the catering. It's a big responsibility, and every year I'm on edge because I fear something will go wrong. Now it has," she said despairingly.

"Are you from this area?" Owen asked.

"No, no, I'm not from Minnesota. I live in Maine. I try to source a different venue every year, somewhere scenic and interesting that writers will be inspired by. There was a big promotion about attracting tourism to this town, which is why I decided to rent one of these houses."

"And when did you arrive?"

"I got here a day before the others, to set things up and supervise the cleaning crew. We were aware the house was very old and atmospheric, but at least needed to give it a good check and make sure it was clean and ready."

"Had anyone been here previously?"

"Well, an earlier group had just left. They were here for a couple of days. Spiritual people, on a silent retreat. So, the place had been used, but it was clean."

"What went wrong? You said there were signs."

Jeanie nodded. "On my first night here, I found out in the morning that someone had broken into my car. The car was empty, and nothing was stolen. It was a rental car, and insured, so I returned it to the car hire company and got a new one. It didn't happen again, but it was still—disturbing, I guess. It definitely made me anxious."

May wondered if the killer had been prowling around, aiming to damage and destroy property before working himself up to more serious crimes.

"Did the police come out to investigate?" Owen asked.

Jeanie shook her head. "No, I didn't call them. I realize now that I should have. But it seemed like a minor thing, although something you'd expect to happen in town, and not out here in such a quiet rural suburb. I called the car rental company and sent them photos, and they said they would organize it with their insurance and do the paperwork. They collected the car and gave me a replacement."

She sighed, raking her fingers through her wild, flyaway hair.

"What exactly did the damage involve?" May asked.

"One of the windows was smashed, and the car's paintwork was damaged."

"Do you have photos of the damage?" Owen asked.

"I do. I can show you if you like," she said.

She scrolled through her phone and found the photos, which she then showed to Owen. He enlarged them and looked closely, his face intent.

May waited hopefully.

"I think we need to go and examine this car," Owen said to May. "I can't tell from the photos, but to me it looks as if there might be something carved into the paintwork. Perhaps it will lead us somewhere."

"I hired it from Bert's Rentals, right here in Cole Hill," Jeanie explained.

"We'll head there now," May said. She didn't think there was anything more to be gained from questioning this group. Nobody had seen or heard anything, and since the group had only arrived the morning after the neighboring victim had been killed, none of the guests could have been the perpetrator.

But this break in was something to pursue. This kind of random crime in such a remote, rural area was certainly unusual. It was raising a red flag for May, and she was eager to find out more.

*

Ten minutes later, after driving out of the scenic countryside and back into the town center of Cole Hill, May and Owen arrived at Bert's Rentals.

The car hire company was small, with a front office on the main street, and a lot at the back of the office where May saw about five rental vehicles of different shapes and sizes were parked. From the photos, Jeanie's car had been dark blue, and she saw a dark blue Ford in a covered parking bay. Perhaps that was the one.

They headed into the office, where a mustached man in his thirties was busy on the phone. As soon as he had finished his call, May approached quickly.

"We're investigating the recent murders in the historic houses, and we're here to see the car that's in your lot," May said. "The one that was broken into."

"I'm Bert," he introduced himself. "I just heard about the murders now, on the morning news. And I sure hope that this can be solved. It's not what you want in a town that relies on tourism, that's for sure. But anyway, you can have a look at the car. The damage is quite extensive. Someone didn't just smash the glass; they really went to town on the paintwork too."

He led them out of the office and into the lot, where he headed over to the car in question, which was the one May had seen.

"You're just in time," he told her as they approached it. "It's booked in for repairs this morning and we're taking it through in an hour."

May was surprised by the extent of the damage. It hadn't just been a side window broken. In fact, the entire driver's window had been smashed to smithereens. The bodywork was dented, but what intrigued May was the silvery-white scratches that had been carved into the car's blue paintwork.

They were a series of symbols that looked a little like hieroglyphics. The crude symbol of a man, a clenched fist, and a drop of something that May guessed, with a stretch of the imagination, could be blood.

"It looks familiar. Why does it look familiar?" Owen asked, sounding puzzled.

"You're right. I've seen something similar before. I'm going to take a clearer photo of it and send it to Sheriff Jack. He might be able to recognize it." May's mind raced as she carefully photographed this strangely familiar design. Then she quickly texted it to Sheriff Jack.

"Does this symbol look familiar?" she messaged. "It was on a car that was vandalized outside the second murder site."

"Thank you," she told Bert, and they headed outside.

As May and Owen walked out, her phone rang. Seeing it was Jack, she quickly picked it up.

"Hello, May. I do recognize the logo," her boss said.

"That's great. Where's it from?" May asked.

"It's a local militia group called Brothers in Blood. They caused some trouble a while ago in Cole Hill, and I remember reading through the case there."

Brothers in Blood. The case wasn't familiar to May, but the name was. These militia members had definitely caused trouble in the past.

"Do you remember the case?"

"They cause trouble continually. Their motto is 'Take Back Our Town' and they're very unwelcoming to the out-of-towners. There have been several reports of militia members threatening tourists in bars, and there was a road rage incident involving a car with out of state plates, and also an incident of vehicle vandalism where one of the militia members got arrested. Cole Hill will have the details because it was in their police department."

"Thank you so much, Jack. We'll get the details now."

May cut the call, feeling excited.

Perhaps Brothers in Blood had decided to take their campaign a step further and escalate it to murder.

CHAPTER SEVEN

Deep in his darkened hiding place, the man who spoke to the dead was listening. He was all alone, in the peace and silence of his retreat, waiting for the voices that he craved.

The dead in this historic district were very vocal, he knew. They were full of stories and information because the area was steeped in such rich history. Some of them spoke in soft, thready voices, while others whispered, like the wind in the trees. Some of them boomed like thunder, but only communicated during storms.

They all had to be listened to. Those who could be understood and were willing to impart valuable information were worth hearing, and he would lock on to them.

But there were also some who expressed themselves in a fevered, garbled fashion, and these were the ones that he often had to work hardest to discern. They were confusing and often upsetting and made it difficult to understand.

But the man who spoke to the dead knew they were there, waiting to be heard.

He had no idea how he was able to do what he did and how he had mastered the craft over the years. But he did have a rare talent, and he knew that it was an invaluable gift. Even though he could never remember, afterward, what the voices said to him, he was convinced that it was important for them to be heard. He tried to write down his memories in a ledger. The voices liked that; he was sure they did.

But the problem was that recently, the man couldn't hear the voices that he needed. He couldn't give them the attention that he knew they craved.

Because now, there were too many other sounds, drowning them out.

He was used to the rustling of leaves, the flapping of wings, and the creaks and groans of the old building. But those sounds didn't matter as he had always been able to shut them out. It was the other sounds that were the problem. The new sounds.

Now, he could hear the hum of cars from a road that had always been much quieter, before the tourists came pushing their way in.

He was deafened by the giggling of the women who walked their dogs past the area where the spirits waited, and he heard their complaints about the mess left by their neighbors. He heard their conversations as they gossiped, and he heard the jingling of their dogs' collars.

As well as all these noises, he also heard a lot of other things, including the distant and muffled sounds of work being carried out in the surrounding homes, where places were being renovated and lived in again.

There were bangs and crashes, the sounds of hammering and drilling. It was impossible to sort through the sounds and filter out the unwanted noise. He knew he had to focus and get rid of the things that were distracting him. He had to make sure that he returned the environment to the way it should be. Dead quiet.

Because the dead needed him.

He breathed in and out, tried to focus, and tried to prepare himself for spending some time with the dead, down in the dark hiding place where he could be close to them.

Just as he was about to tune out this discordant din, he began hearing the thump-thump of music. This was one of the most intrusive sounds, and it made his blood boil. There was loud music being played, and now there were distant bangs that flared up in a discordant boiling of noise.

He clenched his hands, feeling his nails dig into his palms. The dead would be frightened by this; he knew they would be. It was unfair to these ancient spirits. It was totally disrespectful that these other people were coming in with their hammers and drills, blasting and barging their way into the special, sacred area, cutting through layers of history that they knew and cared nothing for.

And as he gritted his teeth, fighting for control over these random, disturbing sounds, he knew that his concentration was being split. He was trying to hear too many things. And he couldn't hear the voices.

The dead were getting anxious. They were not being heard anymore, and he needed to hear their stories.

It was a terrible, tense feeling, not being able to hear the dead. It was as if something rare and precious had suddenly been taken away from him.

And he struggled to hear, and as his ears throbbed with the background noise and the voices fell silent, the man knew that the situation was getting way out of control. He had never thought that this place could be tainted or made filthy by modern constructions and renovations.

But he could still hear the sounds that he knew were coming from next door, and the houses beyond. They were getting louder, and he could even, on occasion, swear he heard the faint sound of splashing water.

He had to put a stop to this! He had to. Only he could do it, the one who listened and heard, who understood, translated, and communicated the strange, fragile noises of the dead. He could feel they were getting anxious, these spirits who resided here. They were becoming nervous and frantic, without the conduit that he provided, and yet his frustration surged again, because he was helpless. He couldn't hear them, even though he tried. There was not enough quietness now to pick up their passing voices, in this area that was so important.

It was a history that could not be ignored.

It was a place where the past was never truly forgotten.

He had to get up and deal with it again. He had to take control. He had to reclaim what was being stolen from him, and he would do it. He would have to purge the area of the new, modern, and intrusive sounds. One by one, he would annihilate the people making this noise.

It was the only way to handle this dreadful intrusion. He knew that he had to take drastic action if he was going to restore peace to these voices. He was not a violent man, but somehow, what he'd done in the past two days had felt right, as if it satisfied something deep in his soul.

It was for the voices, of course. All for the voices.

It was time, he decided. He could not take this for a moment longer. Not for another moment. If he didn't act, if he didn't try to contain the destruction, then who would? There was only one caretaker, only one intermediary. There was only him, the chosen one, the man who heard everything.

He reached out and grabbed his weapon. Heavy and smooth, it fit perfectly in his large hand, and he felt its weight. The end was now bloodied and splintered, but he didn't mind that. The voices didn't mind it either.

They were telling him to go out and make their home safe and peaceful again. Rage boiled inside him, hot and sudden, as he took in the sheer audacity of what these visitors had done and what they had destroyed.

He jotted a quick note into his ledger so that the spirits would be reassured, so that they would know he was out protecting them, fighting for them, killing for them.

"I'm going," he mumbled, standing up and getting ready to exit his secret hideaway, gripping his weapon firmly. He knew where he was headed. "I'm going. It'll all be okay; it'll be quiet again soon. And then, I'll be back to listen."

CHAPTER EIGHT

Owen arrived at the Cole Hill police department five minutes after leaving the car rental offices. As May pulled into the parking lot, he felt eager to see if any local Brothers in Blood militia members had recently caused trouble or been arrested. With only two years of experience in the local police department so far, some details of the local crime landscape were new to him.

A trouble-causing militia based near this scenic town was a huge worry. He could imagine that might cause all kinds of crime. Especially if they had violent tendencies and were perceiving tourists as being invaders of their territory.

Owen knew that such individuals lived by their own rules and had no regard for the law, and the small town of Cole Hill was clearly considered by them to be part of their base and safe zone. He was curious and eager to know if the trouble they caused had increased along with the burgeoning tourism in the area.

Owen wanted to learn what he could while he was here and speaking to the local police.

The Cole Hill police department was small, and it was housed inside a tidy, red-brick building. It had been built in the nineteen thirties, Owen saw, according to a small plaque on the wall. He liked the way that Cole Hill acknowledged all its history. He thought it was a great little town that deserved to capitalize on its tourist potential, without such terrible crimes setting things back.

He followed May into the police department and headed for the front desk.

Owen was sure May would already know the officer on duty, and so it proved. She greeted him with a smile.

"Officer Denver," she said. "This is my partner, Owen Lovell."

Owen felt a surge of pride to be working alongside May, introduced as her partner, as he shook hands with officer Denver.

"I'm pleased to meet you," he said.

"I'm pleased to meet you too," said the officer.

Owen always felt amped to be able to learn from May's competence and the easy way she dealt with people. He guessed she had no idea how well-loved she was in the county, and how much respect she'd gained. Especially since she'd had to deal with a whole series of tough and heartbreaking crimes since becoming deputy, but the way she handled them was simply amazing.

Of course, Owen's emotions were now caught up with her in a different way, and after three dates, he knew that he was falling hard for her. He was starting to think about a future where they were together.

The only glitch in his bright and exciting vision for the future was that, recently, May had been rather offish. It had felt as if she was hiding something from him, or at any rate, not revealing her thoughts.

When he thought about that, he felt a pang of fear that she'd changed her mind or decided to date someone else.

He knew he needed to speak to her about it, but that was a scary prospect. Because it would mean the finality of knowing. Owen didn't know if he was ready for that, and for now, it was easier just not to think about it.

There were more important issues to consider in any case. Like the criminal records of Brothers in Blood members, which May was now asking Denver about.

"We saw an insignia scratched into the paintwork of a rental car whose window was smashed," May was explaining. "Sheriff Jack said it looked a lot like their militia logo, and so we were wondering if you could give us the case history and explain which member of the group was arrested."

"Well, they're sure known for causing trouble here in town," the officer said with a nod. "Many of the militia have had warnings, and we've broken up fights and confrontations from time to time. They don't like the influx of tourists," he explained, confirming what Owen and May had suspected. "They regard them as outsiders and believe that they should keep away from what they call their 'rightful territory'."

"Is that so?" May asked, sounding as interested as Owen felt.

"As for an actual record, let me see who it was."

Owen moved forward, looking at the screen eagerly as the officer checked up on the arrest records for the area.

"Yes. It was one of the core militia members, Colin Dean, who was arrested last year. He was charged with vandalism, smashing up a tourist's rental car and telling him to get the hell out of town because strangers weren't welcome."

Owen's eyes widened. This was eerily similar to what had happened at the retreat the night before last. It could very easily be the same person at work, but now escalating his quest to purge the area of foreigners.

"And the consequences?" May asked.

"He was given a three-month sentence with the option of a fine, and I think he paid the fine. The militia is able to raise funds for its cause, unfortunately. Sadly, they are well subsidized by the people in the area who don't like outsiders."

Owen shook his head. What was up with some people? Sometimes, the peculiarity of folk astounded him. How could you harbor actual dislike—even hatred—for travelers and tourists who brought income to the town, who put it on the world map, who arrived to enjoy a vacation and spend money?

It made total financial sense to welcome the tourists who could add so much to the town, but Owen acknowledged that the thinking of an anti-outsider militia group was going to be very different. He just couldn't put himself in their shoes, no matter how hard he tried to understand them.

Join the twenty-first century, he wanted to say to anyone who felt that way. Join the modern age. Be a decent human being and stop hating on others just for having a different zip code.

"What's Colin's address?" May asked.

"He lives a few miles out of town, on the road going up to the Parkway Forest. I've driven past their place a few times. It's quite an eyesore," the officer said.

"In what way?" Owen asked, wanting to know what they would need to do to prepare. He guessed they would need to be ready for anything when going up against an actual militia.

"It's a big, walled building that looks more like a fortress, but in fact I understand it's the family compound as well as the headquarters of Brothers in Blood. Colin lives there with his brother and sister, and probably a few other people at any given time. Place could use a coat of paint and some attention paid to the front yard." The officer shrugged. "But I guess that's not a priority in their life. I've never been inside, so I've no idea if it's any better than it looks."

"Can you give us the coordinates, please," May said.

"Sure."

The officer wrote them down, and May keyed them into her phone.

"Thank you," she said to him. And then, to Owen, she said, "Let's go visit Colin. If he's a trouble causer who hates outsiders, there's surely a good chance he might have been involved with these killings."

Owen nodded, heading out, feeling resolute at their new lead, but also a little worried. The two were about to go and visit a militia member who might be a killer.

He didn't know much about the local militias, but one fact, inherent in the name itself, was that they were well armed. That was a big worry. Right now, he was uneasily aware that he had no idea what they might end up facing.

He and May were going to be walking into a potentially explosive situation, especially since Owen was sure the only people that the Brothers in Blood hated more than outsiders, was the local police.

CHAPTER NINE

May felt determined, but also very nervous, as she headed along the Parkway Forest road, looking out for the big, walled compound where the coordinates would lead.

She knew this might end up being an aggressive confrontation. Even if Colin Dean proved to be innocent, it was likely to go badly. And May was far from sure that he was innocent. The militia's insignia was a definite link. It wasn't even a vague link. It was a distinct lead, straight to this man, who had a previous conviction for similar vandalism. Had he smashed up Jeanie's car, murdered Marie in the home next door, and then decided, the next night, to come back for more?

There was a clear motive for these killings, and May wondered if the whole group could be in on it.

The fact remained that they were going in to confront a well-armed militia, with the sole purpose of uncovering the truth. This was not going to be easy. But when May thought about the victims, those women who had never had a chance to escape the brutal killing blow, her resolve hardened, and she felt ready to take them on. Whatever it took, this killer must be stopped.

"There it is!" Owen said. "Look, May."

It was set about two hundred yards off the road, up on a hill. It had a high double gate, with dark, narrow windows set in it at intervals. There was a rutted lane leading up to it, and thick bushes surrounding the walls. There seemed to be a path leading through the bushes, and she wondered if the militia used it at night to patrol and protect their compound.

Even though it was daylight, there were no signs of life. But May knew that from the time they turned off that main road, there was a chance they were being watched.

"Here we go," she said in a tight voice, making the turn that she was worried would alert them to their arrival.

She drove down the lane. There was no option to go anything but slow. The road was badly maintained, the ruts deep and rugged. And ahead, the tall, solid gate loomed.

There was a doorbell and an intercom set in it. May didn't like the fact that there was no way of ascertaining who was inside. They couldn't see a thing, but they could be seen.

"Let's take a walk around first," she said.

It wasn't what she had wanted to do. She usually felt more comfortable with the direct approach, simply walking up to the door, armed with the knowledge that she was investigating a crime and representing the law.

But here, this high-walled and threatening building was impenetrable, and May wanted to examine all her options. Perhaps there was another way in, or a better line of sight from behind the place. So far, nobody had come out to confront them, and she couldn't see any cameras, so for now, perhaps they were not aware the police had arrived.

May and Owen headed along the path, taking in the extent of this strange compound. The right-hand side of it was fully walled, but as they reached the back of the large walled area, probably a couple of acres in size, she saw another gate, this one a steel-barred gate, that led onto a dirt road winding its way up into the forest.

Wondering if she could get an actual glimpse inside, May peeked through the bars, but there was nothing to be seen except the wall of a nearby barn, and a couple of dilapidated trucks parked nearby. Tire tracks led into the barn.

"It seems like someone's at home," May observed.

"But it doesn't look like there's much activity going on," Owen said.

May agreed. For sure, someone was inside, but perhaps it was a slow day here at the Brothers in Blood compound. If so, that would be lucky for them.

They had still seen nobody. Not a soul. She was beginning to feel thoroughly unsettled by this outing, so far removed from what she usually came across in terms of her policing. There was something very threatening about this vast, still, walled area, in which she knew that the normal rules of society might be tossed into the trash can.

She glanced at Owen. He was looking around, his eyes sharp and alert, as they reached the third side of the square compound.

They were vigilant. They were ready for anything. Trying to summon all her confidence, May decided that she was going to refuse to be intimidated by this setup. She had to remain professional. She had a job to do. She was here to get justice for two innocent victims, and hopefully prevent any further lives from being claimed.

So, coming back to the big steel main gate on the front wall, she rang the buzzer and waited. There were footsteps approaching. She could hear them, quick and regular. Then both she and Owen jumped simultaneously as they heard the click-click of metal that May associated with a weapon being primed.

But it was not a gun. It was only the metallic sound of the gate being opened from inside, probably by unfastening a big steel latch.

To May's surprise, a woman stepped out.

She was dressed in beige pants, black boots, and a camouflage jacket with the letters "BB" and a logo on the pocket. May looked closely at it. Without a doubt, this was the same handiwork that had been so crudely scratched into the car's bodywork.

She had a large machine gun slung over her shoulder and she regarded May and Owen without a trace of warmth.

"What do you want?" she asked.

May felt sure that she already knew at least part of the reason why two police had arrived at her front door.

"We need to question Colin Dean," May said firmly.

"Why's that?" the woman asked.

"Are you his sister?" May countered with another question.

"I am his sister."

"What's your name?"

May and Owen both tensed again, as a rattle from nearby split the silence. But it was just a black trash bag, blown by the wind, buffeting against the gatepost. For a moment it had sounded just like running footsteps.

May found herself doubting her first impression. Had it been running footsteps? Had someone been listening from inside one of the buildings, and then made a run from the window—possibly to get a weapon? May shivered inwardly. She was not getting a good feeling about standing here.

"My name's Petal," the woman replied.

"Your birth name?" May asked, surprised.

"Yup. Petal Dean," she said, not looking happy about it. "I've been meaning to change it. But that involves dealing with government." She grimaced.

Petal? May felt briefly incredulous. Petal's mother had clearly never dreamed that, someday, her daughter would form part of a core team of militia. If she had, she was sure she'd have chosen a different name, a more aggressive one.

"Petal, we want to question Colin in connection with a crime in Cole Hill. A series of crimes, actually. Is he here?"

"He's no criminal."

"He has a record," May pointed out. She wasn't looking to start a fight, but she had to state facts and justify her presence on the unwelcoming doorstep of this compound. "He was arrested after vandalizing a rental vehicle belonging to a tourist. We're investigating a crime where a vehicle was vandalized in a similar way, and a short while later, a murder occurred."

Was it May's imagination, or did the woman's eyes widen suddenly?

"I think you're picking on us," she retorted. "It's just another example of police prejudice."

May's eyes widened at this unfair comment, but Petal was now in full flood.

"We didn't have anything to do with the vandalism. It was a wrongful arrest. We can't be held responsible if people copy our insignia. It's not like it's copyrighted, you know. People idolize us. A lot of people in this area agree with our beliefs, that strangers mean trouble—crime and interference—and that in this area, we should keep to ourselves."

She said the last words in a loud, passionate tone. May half expected Petal to fling her fist in the air. Glancing at Owen, she saw he was looking carefully at the slits in the building above, and May wondered if he'd spied movement there. They needed to be careful. If someone from inside began taking pot shots at them to scare them off, they'd need to react fast.

"Petal, we're here on a murder investigation. This is not police bullying. And you haven't answered my question."

"What question?" Petal retorted.

"Is Colin here?"

Petal shrugged. "I'm not responsible for him. How should I know where he is?"

"This is his recorded address and your militia headquarters. So, I'm sure you do know," May insisted, wondering why the sister was being so obstructive. To her, it pointed to guilt.

And then, she and Owen jumped again as the loud sound of automatic gunfire resounded through the air. May felt her heart accelerate. The worst had happened. They were being fired at.

But hot on the heels of her moment of terror, common sense asserted itself. The sound was not gunfire. It was only because she'd been so on edge that she'd thought that way. It was a car exhaust, doing a massive rapid backfire.

The scream of an engine followed.

And in a flash, May realized she'd gone off on the wrong tangent completely. They were not in any danger of being shot here—at any rate, not now. That had not been the reason why Petal had arrived at the gate, with her questions and delaying tactics.

They were in danger of losing their suspect, because while they'd been trying to get in the main gate, the man they were looking for had sped out of the back. That car noise had been close by. There could be no other place it had come from.

And to confirm her suspicions, she saw a sudden shadow of relief cross Petal's face, as if she'd also heard the car depart and knew she'd done her job.

Colin was not planning on shooting but fleeing. And he'd done it. He'd fled.

And now, to catch up, May was going to have to chase this suspect down, at top speed.

CHAPTER TEN

May felt frantic that she'd been outmaneuvered by Petal's rhetoric and delaying tactics.

"It's him, and he's running," she hissed to Owen. "Stay here! Don't let Petal get away! We need her if we can't get the others!"

Having issued the emergency instructions to try and save this disaster, May turned and bolted for her car.

She felt stunned that despite the militia's intimidating setup, the intention on Colin Dean's side had never been to fight, but rather to flee.

It was a clear indication of guilt, but May was hugely worried about what might happen if this man managed to make a clean getaway. She had no doubt there were enough of his supporters in the area that he would be able to disappear, hidden away from May and Owen because, in the militia's mindset, the police were the enemy.

Jumping into the driver's seat, she started the car and hit the gas, slewing down the track with wheels spinning.

May didn't think it would be possible for this man to hide out forever, but she was pretty sure he could do it for long enough for the mayor to get seriously mad at the police and make good on his promises of retribution.

Now, she had to find a way to get onto that back road. She hoped that if she drove farther down this track, there would be a route that would allow her to catch up to him.

Frustration surged inside her at the thought that they might lose this precious lead. It would be so easy to get away in what had sounded like a big, powerful ATV. So, she had to focus. She had to catch this man. It was literally a make-or-break scenario, and she knew the stakes couldn't be higher.

Trying to ignore the bumps and potholes that were jolting her right out of her seat, May sped down the rough track, breathing a silent apology to her poor car for this abusive treatment.

To her relief, there was a side road, just as rough, but it led to a dirt road beyond that was the exit route from the compound's back gate.

There he was! Her instincts had been right. As the car slewed around the track, she saw the trail of dust from the large, dirty-white ATV that had burst from out of the compound.

The vehicle was fishtailing down the road at top speed and even though he had a good lead on her, May thought she could hear the engine screaming. This man now had a massive advantage. He was in a better vehicle for the terrain, he knew the area, and he had all the motivation to get away.

May grabbed the radio.

"I need backup! Backup required. I'm chasing down a suspect who's fleeing on the dirt road leading to Parkway Forest," she gabbled breathlessly.

"Copy that. We'll try and get a car there," the Cole Hill operator replied.

Then there was no time to do anything but focus on this bumpy, spine-jarring ride as she accelerated at dangerous speeds along this slippery, sandy trail. It was all she could do to keep the departing dust cloud in sight.

"Come on, May!" she urged herself. "Come on, come on! You can catch him."

She crested a small hill, her car briefly airborne and then bouncing down on the road again. There was a short stretch of level ground ahead. There, she gunned the engine, trying to push it as fast as it could go. She saw the ATV in the distance again, clearly now, jolting over the ground.

He was pulling away fast. He was probably a mile away from the compound and making good time. Where was he heading to? Perhaps, he was going to try and reach one of his supporters out in the forest?

May knew there was a strong chance she was chasing down a killer on the run, and he could be a danger to anyone who came across his path. But she realized that in his panic, the driver ahead of her was wasting time. He was oversteering, gunning the engine to a scream, and spinning his wheels. This was not a cool, calm, or collected man.

His panic was slowing him down, while in contrast, May was doing everything she could to keep a controlled mindset, despite the adrenaline-spiking circumstances.

Ahead, the trail narrowed, running in between ranks of pine trees, and May gasped as the ATV slewed left and then right, skidding in a pile of loose sand, coming within a hair's breadth of crashing into the left-hand trees. But somehow, in this crisis situation, the driver that she knew must be Colin Dean managed to keep the ATV on the road.

That had slowed him down some, she saw. He'd realized he had survived a near crash. After such a close call, he was being more cautious. May hoped it had also dented his confidence. The crazed panic of his flight seemed to her to be slowing slightly.

"I can do this," May told herself. She needed to believe she could. She was a good driver. This might not be the right car for the job, but she'd spent her life cruising along back roads like these. She could read them; she understood them. Even though the frenzied chase was slippery and dangerous, and the road was so rough she could just about feel the top of her spine connecting with her skull.

But what she did know was that she was catching up. She was now within a couple of hundred yards of the fleeing man, and she could see she was getting closer. In fact, she could see him now, a dark shape behind the wheel. In fact, May now picked up there were two shapes in the car. So, Colin must be fleeing with his brother.

They'd both decided to make the quick getaway, leaving their sister behind to stall the police.

She had no doubt that he was spending far too much time looking in his mirror. That would also make his flight less effective.

What could she do to build on the advantage she thought she was slowly clawing in?

Intimidation, May thought. This chase was a mental game. He was now on the back foot. He'd made errors already, had a few close calls. He had to choose the route ahead whereas all she had to do was follow. He was under pressure and the fear of the chase was getting to him.

So, put him under more pressure, May thought. And luckily, she had the perfect equipment to do it!

Flicking the switches, she turned on her lights and siren, knowing that she was close enough for the brothers to hear and see both. The police pursuit would now be a scary reality, hopefully making her seem even more threatening.

With a flare of triumph, May saw her tactic had worked.

He'd definitely slowed. Her actions had given him a moment of sheer panic. The assault of lights and noise had thrown him off his stride. Ahead, she saw his vehicle veer and skid.

He was losing it, May thought. He was looking behind him, he was worried about being chased.

"That's it! That's it! Slow down! Slow down!" she urged him.

Then, with a roar, the ATV driver made a decision and swerved hard to the left. He was heading down a track that looked almost impassable. As she reached it, May hit the brakes.

She couldn't follow down here. It was narrow, rutted, and deeply eroded. But as she stared, confused, she realized it didn't seem to lead anywhere. It wound away into the forest, more like a dried-up river bed than a road.

Never mind that she couldn't follow. He couldn't get anywhere. This road was undrivable. He'd taken a shortcut that had led nowhere.

He'd made a fatal error. In fact, as the car spun its wheels over a thick patch of sand, May now saw the two men inside were arguing with each other. The man in the passenger side looked to be attacking the driver, punching him, and shaking him. Clearly, he blamed his brother for the bad decision and was venting his rage.

The car rocked and swayed. The wheels spun again.

They were getting stuck, May saw. They were getting stuck, and this meant that she finally had a chance.

"They've turned off on a sidetrack. Their vehicle is lodged in the sand," she radioed breathlessly, updating the control room on the latest twist in this chase.

Now was the most dangerous part of the pursuit, May knew. Desperate and cornered, these two men might reach for their weapons. She had to get ahead of the game, while the brothers were attacking each other and trying to maneuver their car out of the clinging, uneven sand. Now was the only chance she had to take the advantage.

May jumped out of her car and sprinted toward the mired ATV, her own shoes sinking into the sand, staggering as she ran but not letting it slow her down.

She got her gun out and held it at the ready. And then, she burst past the ATV, standing in front of it, aiming her gun at the two men through the windshield, with a steady hand.

"Get out of the vehicle!" she yelled breathlessly. "Get out! Hands in the air! Now! Or I will shoot."

The two bearded men stared at her in utter shock. There was a moment where she thought the driver tried to reach for his own gun, and her adrenaline spiked again. Then the passenger punched his arm and yelled something that sounded like, "Are you mad?"

"I will shoot!" May screamed, pressing home her advantage.

She saw the driver capitulate, shaking his head, clearly deciding that she meant what she said.

Reluctantly, the two men climbed out of the car with their hands in the air. On the track she'd just turned off, May heard the shrill sound of sirens approaching. Backup had arrived, and now the two fleeing brothers could be arrested.

May couldn't wait to question them and hoped that she would be able to keep up the pressure, crack through their defenses and prove their guilt in the shortest possible time.

CHAPTER ELEVEN

After the breakneck speed of the chase through the forest, May was shaking all over with tension and the aftermath of the ride. But she knew that the most challenging part of this pursuit was still to come. It would be questioning these two men, who had chosen to flee, and who clearly had no respect or trust for the police.

She walked into the Cole Hill police department, where the suspects had been taken, shoulder to shoulder with Owen, hoping for a successful outcome.

"Afternoon, deputies. We've got the men in the interview room, waiting. Would you like to interview them together or separately?" the officer asked.

"Together, for now. We can separate them if we need to?" May questioned Owen, who nodded in confirmation that this was the best way forward.

"These guys are going to resist us all the way, I have no doubt," she muttered to Owen.

"We're going to need to lean hard on them," he agreed.

In the background, May could hear the thud and boom of loud rock music. There seemed to be a concert near the historic area, down by the lake, and although it was about a mile away, the sound was traveling.

It felt like a dramatic backdrop to this important questioning, but May just hoped that the interview room was well soundproofed. She didn't want the noise to cause a disturbance.

But as she headed down the corridor, something else caused a disturbance.

Her phone began ringing loudly, and May saw it was her mother calling.

It seemed rude to let it go to voicemail. Instead, May decided to pick up quickly and explain the stressful circumstances she was in, even though she knew she would risk getting embroiled in a conversation that would raise her blood pressure still further.

"Mom," she said, turning aside and speaking in a low voice.

"May! I have to ask you. Have you heard about these murders?" her mother asked.

"Yes, of course I have! We're busy now, very busy, working on the case," May said. "I'm actually at the police department now, about to go into the interview room to question someone."

Her mother didn't get the hint.

"Oh, I'm so glad to hear it! I was surprised that your boss hasn't already called in the FBI, because this is obviously very serious. I was wondering if I should call Kerry and ask her if she'd like to come for dinner, seeing she might be here soon."

May felt her tension rising. It had been a bad idea to pick up this call.

"Not yet," she said through gritted teeth. The unspoken comparison riled her. "The FBI is not yet called in."

"You know, I have a close friend, Edna, who knows the historic district really well," her mother continued.

"Mom—" May tried, but Mrs. Moore seemed temporarily unstoppable.

"She was the one who called me and told me about what happened. She's very much in the loop with the activities in the area, you see. She's been involved in a lot of the renovations because she knows the background to these old homes, she has researched a lot of the plans. It's quite fascinating, really. She's a lovely lady."

"Mom—" May said again. This was not the time!

"We actually met about twenty years ago at the local fair. So, we have been friends for ages, simply ages."

"I really have to go. My suspect is waiting. I'd love to talk about this at a different time," May said breathlessly, returning Owen's worried gaze.

"I know, I know. You do sound busy, angel. But what I wanted to tell you is that Edna is available. I am sure she could be a very knowledgeable connection. She might even help you solve this! So, if you want her number, or you want me to arrange a coffee meeting or something similar, I'll do that! And let me know if Kerry's in town, won't you, sweetheart?"

"I absolutely will. Thanks, Mom. I appreciate the news on Edna. She sounds like a very helpful person. That history must be fascinating. Give Dad a hug. Speak later."

May disconnected, feeling totally thrown thanks to this call, which had gotten all her insecurities flaring. And now she had to go in and interview two dangerous and recalcitrant suspects. The timing could not be worse.

Feeling more stressed than ever, May pushed open the interview room door and walked inside, with Owen behind her.

This was the first time May had gotten an up-close and personal look at the two suspects, while not aiming a weapon at them. It was clear they were brothers, and she could see the family resemblance to Petal also.

The man sitting on the left, who had been in the passenger seat, had been IDed as Colin's brother, Mitch. He had a greasy head of hair that seemed to have been styled to look unwashed and a biker's beard. On his right arm, he had a poorly done tattoo of a snake, and on his left arm he had the militia's insignia tattooed.

In contrast, Colin himself looked fitter and was taller. He had a shock of thick, black hair and a well-trimmed beard. Both of them were staring defiantly at May with identical piercing blue eyes.

She closed the door. To her relief, the noise of the rock concert was now almost inaudible, nothing more than a subsonic boom.

"Colin Dean. Mitch Dean," May addressed them. "We're police deputies and we are questioning you regarding recent crimes in Cole Hill."

"What crimes are you talking about? We know nothing about any crimes!" Colin snapped at her. May sensed that he was angry to have been bested by a police officer and a woman at that. All his resistance was in place again.

"A vehicle outside one of the historic homes on Windrush Road was vandalized, and your organization's insignia was carved into the paintwork," May said sternly. "That night, a visitor in the home next door was killed. The next night, in the other home, murder was committed and another out of town woman was killed."

Colin drew his breath in briefly. May thought he looked momentarily appalled. Then he shrugged. "I know nothing about the murders. And I can't help it if people admire our militia."

"You were convicted for the same vandalism crime a while ago."

"Copycat crime, clearly," he said sullenly.

"Two visitors to the area were murdered," May said. "That's not a copycat crime."

"Look, I'm sorry to hear this. I really am. I'm not some kind of monster that takes pleasure in hearing about these things," Colin insisted, jutting his chin. "You might think I am, but you're wrong. We did not have anything to do with the murders. We're not a criminal organization. We might make the occasional statement, to send a message, but we're not thugs and killers. The crime comes from the outsiders, the visitors, and this has just proven it."

"What?" Owen asked incredulously.

"Isn't it obvious? They came to town and look, they were murdered! This just reinforces my theory that if there were no strangers here, there would be no crime!"

May thought her brain might explode as she tried to take in that warped logic. No wonder the militia was gaining followers in the area from people who liked the sound of words they didn't have to think too hard about, she realized.

"It's not the visitors' fault that they were murdered. It's the killer's fault, and that's why you're here. Because you are a strong suspect," May pressured him. "You do realize that your militia's insignia on the vehicle is a very strong link to this crime? Plus, you fled when we arrived and that only adds to the proof. You are showing very clear signs of guilt and based on this evidence and your own actions, we could arrest you and charge you with this murder immediately!"

May glared at them. She knew she needed to present a tough, strong front. These men would only respect her if she did that. And right now, she needed them to be scared.

It was strange, she realized, how coming across as so aggressive and assertive actually made her feel as if she could be that way, deep inside. As if she could be as much of a badass as her sister Kerry, given the chance. Maybe even more of a badass.

And the men now looked intimidated, she realized with a flare of satisfaction. They were glancing at each other in a worried way.

Mitch cleared his throat. "We're law-abiding citizens. You just don't understand us, do you? We're known in the area for a reason. We do good work. We help police the outlying areas, you know, where the police never have time to go."

May raised her eyebrows inwardly. More like, areas where the police were not accepted or invited because the militia had fomented distrust, she thought.

"We didn't do this crime. We don't approve of killing anyone," Colin said. His tone was now politer.

"But you have no problem with destroying property?" May pointed out. "The problem I have is that when people embrace a cause at all costs, things often escalate. I believe that's what has happened here. You started off by warning people off, and then you decided that murder was a far more effective deterrent than a damaged car."

"No!" Now Colin was pale. "You've gotten the wrong impression of me, I promise! I was feeling bad about the car. Honestly, when you arrived, I thought you'd come to accuse me of vandalizing the car. I had no idea about a murder!"

She could see from his face that he now realized the full extent of the potential trouble. And more importantly, he'd just admitted to being there on the night. She had a confession for the vandalism.

"Then tell me the truth. And this time, I want the truth," May insisted. "What time did you vandalize the car the night before last?"

Colin hung his head. "I—look, I was passing by, at about eight p.m. I saw the car outside that home, and yes, it occurred to me that I could—could issue a statement to back up our beliefs. So, I did smash the window and scrape the paintwork. But then I left!"

"Where did you go?"

"I went to the local bar in Cole Hill. I was on the way there after spending the day fishing."

"Did you see anyone else around?" she asked, wondering if he might have spied the killer, assuming he was telling her the truth.

"No, there wasn't anyone nearby. If there had been, I wouldn't have done what I did!" he protested.

May shook her head. She wasn't convinced by this alibi, even though the second murder had probably occurred later than eight p.m. Colin could easily have come back, on his way back from the bar.

"And last night?" she said. That was when the second murder had occurred, and this would hopefully make or break his alibi.

"We held our weekly meeting last night. It started at six p.m. at the local brewery."

"You hold meetings at the brewery?" Owen asked.

"They have a big room there. We bring the chairs," Colin explained. "It's convenient, as it's close to our headquarters. We arrived earlier to get all the banners in place and set up the snacks. So, we were there from about four in the afternoon. The meeting lasted until ten, and we then carried on drinking with the brewery owner and a few other militia members until sunrise. We were discussing our organization's ideals," he emphasized. "Not just drinking the night away. Mitch and I got home at around six this morning, and caught a couple of hours of shuteye, and then you arrived."

"Can you prove that?" Owen asked.

"The brewery owner can definitely vouch for us. His name's Philip Turk. And also, there is a camera outside the building. So, there would be footage of our cars arriving and leaving."

May shook her head, thinking of the DUI offenses that had most likely been committed. She made a mental note to ask the local police to do more late night and early morning patrols near that brewery on the meeting days.

In terms of alibis, if this checked out, then the Dean brothers were cleared. However, she was still going to hand them over to the local police to pursue the vandalism charges. Actions had to have consequences, and these brothers needed to learn it the hard way.

And, at that moment, May's phone beeped. She glanced down at it, feeling worried to see that a message had come in from Sheriff Jack.

Quickly, she opened it.

"There's been another murder," he had texted her. "As soon as you're done with your interview, you need to get to the scene. A woman's been killed at number seven Pastoral Road, near the lake."

May's heart plummeted. The worst had happened. The killer had struck again.

Another life had been lost, and they were still no closer to knowing who he was. She now needed to get to the crime scene and fast.

CHAPTER TWELVE

May and Owen hit the gas, speeding along the road in the direction of the historic district. May's stomach was churning with stress. She felt terrible that another life had been lost. In fact, she felt responsible, as if there surely must have been something she could have done to stop it.

"He's killing so fast, one victim every night," Owen said in a hushed voice. "May, this is such a disaster. I hope that he's been careless this time."

"We desperately need to stop this. Now," May agreed. Her mouth felt dry. But as she drove, she tried to gather her frantic thoughts, and consider what was known to them already.

This killer was clearly basing his murders around the historic district, which was only a few blocks in size, but the various blocks were separated by a park and a river.

Why was he doing this, she wondered. What was it about that area that was triggering him to kill? Did he live nearby? Did he have some connection with this area?

She needed to explore all these possible lines of investigation. The right one could get her further. But for now, she was pulling up outside the crime scene where, already, several police cars were parked.

As they hurried over to number seven Pastoral Road, which was on the corner of Windrush, and just a couple of blocks from the other affected homes, May's heart thumped with anxiety. A cluster of onlookers had surrounded the yellow crime scene tape. She could see their distressed faces and hear the snippets of shocked conversation as she hurried quickly toward the scene. A couple of the onlookers were crying, and May felt sure that they must be friends or family of the deceased.

She stopped at the doorway to pull on gloves and foot covers, and then, taking a deep breath, walked up the stairs and onto the porch.

The first thing she noticed was that the front door had clearly been forced. It was hanging off its hinges, the lock splintered.

"It's the first sign of forced entry we've seen," Owen observed in a low voice, and May nodded. She didn't know if it was significant, but perhaps it might be.

A police officer from Cole Hill met her inside the home's gracious hallway. His hat was askew on his head and his eyes were panicked.

"Deputy Moore, this is such a disaster. This home was hired for a family gathering. Cressida Brown, the family's great-aunt, stayed behind as she had a headache when the rest of the family went to see the rock concert."

"And?" May asked.

He gestured to the lounge. "It looks as if she fell asleep on the sofa, and he must have broken in and hit her on the head while she was sleeping! She just never woke up. It's too terrible."

May swallowed, feeling sick to her stomach. This was awful. All because she was unlucky enough to be in the home at the wrong time. The atmosphere was thick with tragedy.

It was a tastefully decorated family lounge. The walls were covered with old fashioned wallpaper and there were antique-style furniture and throw rugs. A large fire was laid, ready for the evening, in the fireplace.

May stepped into the room, and her heart was wrenched as she looked at the elderly woman lying on her side on the sofa.

She looked strangely peaceful and had clearly not known a thing before she died. But that meant the likelihood of finding any evidence was small. May could see it had most likely been the same weapon used. The head injury was identical to the other two she'd seen, and there was a splinter of white-painted wood lying next to the corpse. She wondered if he might be placing these splinters there on purpose, and again wondered if this meant there was a link in his mind between the homes and the killings.

May bowed her head, feeling sorrowful and guilty that this had happened. Now, she would have to embark on the difficult job of speaking to the family, to see if anyone might possibly have heard or seen something.

"Could you ask the family members to come through into the hallway?" she said, wanting to speak somewhere private that was not within sight of the murder scene.

"I'll do that," he said.

May headed into the hall with Owen, and a minute later, the police officer ushered six people inside.

"This is the family of Cressida Brown. Her niece, her nephew, his wife, her granddaughter, her second cousin and his wife," he explained.

"I'm so sorry this has happened," May said to the assembled family members.

"We went out to the concert," the niece said, tears rolling down her face. "This was supposed to be a family gathering and now it's a murder scene!"

"What time did you leave for the concert?" May asked.

"We left at about one p.m. We walked down there. And we got back about half an hour ago," the niece explained.

May was glad she now had a more accurate time frame for when the killer had struck. There was a two-hour window when he'd been in the area and able to strike. This would be important when they hopefully caught a suspect. But it was also troubling that this killer was growing bolder. This time, he had killed in broad daylight.

"Did any of you hear anything unusual when you came back?" May asked. "Or see something suspicious either before you left or when you returned?"

"Well, we obviously saw the door was broken, so we were immediately worried," the second cousin—a tall, gray-haired man—said. "We walked inside and saw there had been a crime. I immediately called the police and checked outside to see if there was anyone around, or any signs that someone had been here. I'm an ex-police officer myself, so I know the protocols," he said sadly.

May nodded. With an ex-police officer on the scene, she was sure that if the killer had been lurking nearby, he would have been seen.

He hadn't been. He had been able to come and go, melting into the darkness of night, after claiming an innocent victim.

"How long have you been staying here?" she asked.

"This is our second night," the niece replied.

"Did you experience any difficulty with any locals? Any problems with anyone in the area?" May asked.

She shook her head. "We didn't really connect with any of the locals. We had all our own food and drink. The first time we went out was to the concert. We never even saw anyone from the neighboring houses. The police told us that there were visitors staying there in any case, not locals. One family had just moved out, and another had just moved in, but I believe they're leaving now. They're scared to stay, and I don't blame them. We're going back home too, of course."

May nodded reluctantly. The murder scene was a dead end. She could see that. It seemed unlikely that this time, the killer had been careless.

"I'm so sorry for your loss," she said to the family. "Thank you for your time."

"So, we're still no closer to knowing why he's doing this," Owen muttered as they left.

May shook her head. She felt even more determined to catch this killer and to get answers.

"We're not giving up on this," she said. "And I know it's getting late, but I'm not ready to go home."

"Me either," Owen agreed. "We need to make every minute count. I'll work through the night if that's what it will take."

May felt glad of his resolve, which was motivating her to push even harder in this challenging case.

"I promised the mayor we'd try to solve it tonight. I hope I didn't make a promise we can't keep because we're no further ahead yet. Let's go to the Cole Hill police department and base ourselves there for a while. We can look at all the cases, all the locations, and see what we can find that provides a common thread," she said.

"Good idea," Owen agreed.

They climbed in the car and set off for the short drive to the Cole Hill police department, with May feeling determined that they were going to find the crucial detail they needed.

But, as she reached the police department, her heart sank.

Sheriff Jack's car was there and parked next to it was another car that she recognized from earlier, which made her heart sink.

This was Mayor Tillman's sleek, black ride.

Undoubtedly, the mayor was inside, and May had no doubt he would be spitting mad. In fact, from the stairs, she could already hear loud, shouted words, and she glanced uneasily at Owen.

The timing could not be worse. They had made no progress, they hadn't caught the killer, and worst of all, the historic district had now been struck again. They were going to be heading into an explosive situation, and she had no idea what damage the fallout would cause.

Taking a deep breath, knowing this confrontation would test her in every way, May walked inside.

CHAPTER THIRTEEN

Immediately she set foot in the police department, May knew that this encounter with Mayor Tillman was not going to be as bad as she had feared it would be.

No, it was going to be far worse.

Bright red in the face, the mayor was yelling at Sheriff Jack as if he was standing twenty yards away, rather than two feet.

"I am the mayor of Cole Hill. I demand that you hand me full control of the police department," Mayor Tillman ranted. "Since you have been in charge, we have become a laughingstock! This is nothing but a farce! I want you to pack your bags and get out of my town. I will make sure your position is advertised nationally."

Jack took a step forward and May winced, ready for him to be punched in the face, but luckily the mayor was too surprised by his actions to respond in time.

"Listen, Mayor," he said in a calm voice. "You are right to be extremely concerned about this. So are we. But it's going to take more time to solve this case, especially since this killer is clearly extremely local, and there has been no similar crime in the area in recent times."

"Oh, is that what they told you?" Mayor Tillman sneered. "Listen to me, Sheriff, I can see excuses for what they are. This is pure and simple police incompetence, and it is going to stop now, or I am going to make sure you will be out of a job. You had better come up with a result, and I mean immediately. Because if you don't, I will make sure that you're running your own country road store in no time!"

"Mayor, we have a top-class police force here. They are doing their best to chase down the murderer and they are doing their best to keep the town safe."

"Not their best!" the mayor shouted. "They have failed to eliminate the murderer or give us any leads. In fact, I should be demanding your resignation as sheriff now! You've had your chance!"

"Mayor, no!" May said, appalled.

Being briefly unable to keep her mouth shut was definitely not the wisest career move, May realized a nanosecond later, because now Mayor Tillman was turning to her, his eyes just about popping out of his head with rage.

"There has been no crime in this area for decades. This town has been a paradise, and now it has been spoiled by a terrible villain. And all this has happened just a few months after you were promoted to county deputy? Are you the one who's been letting things slide so badly?"

May winced at that low blow as the mayor continued. "Don't try and convince me that you're doing a good job."

"Mayor, I am capable of doing my job. I've been working on this case all day."

"Oh really?" the mayor inquired, spreading his arms wide. "So where is the murderer now? This is the third victim, and we have no lead. And it just so happens that you're in charge of the investigation. Does that not seem suspicious to you?"

"Mayor, you surely can't believe that I am covering up for the killer?" May demanded, feeling angry now. She was all for resolving conflict, but this criticism was totally unfounded, and he should not be allowed to insult her this way.

He shrugged. "I'm saying that I don't trust you! Or your training! Or your management! If this is not solved by tonight, as you promised, then I'm not going to hold myself back anymore."

He was holding himself back? May sensed Owen looking at him incredulously at those words. But now Tillman continued with a definite note of threat in his tone. "This is your responsibility. You were placed here to keep us safe. And I want you to pay for your failure!"

It took all of May's self-control not to respond emotionally. She couldn't believe how upsetting this was. The mayor was totally out of line. He was abusing his position and being unrealistic in his expectations.

But the problem was that they hadn't solved the case. So ultimately, his criticism would be heard by the higher powers if he chose to escalate it, and it was very clear he was going to do exactly that.

"Mayor, we're doing everything we can," Jack said, and May knew he was speaking out just to get the angry man's attention focused on him again. "But we have to be realistic. Look, the suspect seems to be a local. That's why it's possible that he has been able to hide the evidence of his comings and goings. It's likely that he knows the town well. He is most likely an insider."

"There's surely no way a local could commit these vile crimes," the mayor insisted, shaking his head.

"We need to get to the heart of this case. And the only way we will do that is to get to know our killer, which will help us to identify a motive. That's what my deputy and my team are doing. So please, do give us some more time. It will be well used," Jack said.

With an angry snort, Mayor Tillman turned and marched out, slamming the police department door so hard the whole lobby seemed to shake.

May stared at Jack in concern. Her boss sighed.

"Interference always makes things more difficult, May, but the problem is that he's very influential. He got to this position by being well-connected. So, we need to move on this. We need to get this killer. Or I know that he's going to try to make good on his threats," Jack said.

"We're here to look for a new angle," May promised. "We're going to compare notes on all the cases now and see if there's anything we've missed so far. I hope we will come up with something, Jack, but I guarantee you, we're not going to stop working tonight until we've got the right suspect."

"I have faith in you, May. I'm going to go into a press conference now. I know you're going to give this all you have," Jack said.

He turned and walked out, and May regarded Owen in concern. The stakes had just gotten sky high. Thanks to this angry mayor, their careers were undoubtedly on the line.

"We need to look for common threads," she said, heading into the back room with Owen. Quickly, she opened her laptop and searched through the information they had.

"You know, the factor that seems to play the biggest part here is the geographical area," May said. "All these kills have taken place close by. Do you think that this killer is perceiving the area as his territory? Could he be connected with it in some way and have a background here?"

"If so, what kind of person would he be?" Owen said, wrinkling his forehead in thought. "Perhaps a homeowner who went bankrupt?"

"Yes. Or someone who was living here and got evicted?" May suggested. "There have been a lot of changes recently with the renovation of the area. A lot of people moving in and out, places being cleared, takeovers and sales. Let's focus on both those options."

"Finding an angry ex-tenant, or a squatter that got evicted, or a bankrupt homeowner? I like all those ideas," Owen said.

Now working with the intensity of severe pressure, May accessed the case files, while Owen turned his attention to any bankruptcies and repossessions in the area.

They worked in frantic silence for a few minutes.

And then, May gave a triumphant gasp. At last, her scrutiny of the area's historic crimes had come up with a result she could use.

"Look, Owen!" she said. "Look here. I've found someone. And on reading this case, I can see why he might have a very strong motive for wanting to kill!"

CHAPTER FOURTEEN

May scrutinized the case file through narrowed eyes. She was sure, sure that this criminal might have some answers to give them.

"All the pieces seem to fit together," Owen observed.

And rereading, May couldn't see many drawbacks in their newest suspect.

His name was Dale Crain. He had been a resident of the area for over eight years but had been evicted from a historic house after failing to pay his rent. As they scrolled through the details and documents captured online, May saw it had been a very ugly affair.

"He was a squatter—this house was bought by a property developer that wanted to renovate it. However, Dale, who had moved into the house a few years ago, and had been living rent-free for a few months during the sale, refused to move out when he was served with eviction papers. He started damaging the property and threatening the new owners," May explained. "What makes this case really interesting is that the house he occupied was slap bang in the middle of the historic area that is being targeted," she said to Owen, feeling as if this case had just taken a giant step forward.

"And he didn't stop with threatening. It says here that he actually attacked the new owner with a hammer when he arrived one day with a legal letter demanding that he move. Dale was screaming that this was his home, that no out-of-towners were allowed to live here, and that nobody was going to move him out," Owen read, seemingly hypnotized by the details.

"There are a lot of parallels here," May agreed.

"He went to prison for two years. And he was paroled just a few weeks ago. So that time frame would definitely make sense."

A paroled criminal, out in society for a few weeks, was top of the list in terms of suspects.

"But where's Dale living now?" May asked.

That seemed to be a stumbling block. Owen went back into a different database and searched frantically.

"Why no address?" he said, letting out a frustrated sigh.

"Sometimes, data is just missing. He could have moved and not been updated by the parole department. There's often a delay in recording the new address," May said. But now she was wondering if this ducking and diving could have been intentional, even planned, so that Dale Crain would not be found when the police went hunting.

"So, how are we going to find him?" Owen asked. "There must be a way."

May thought over the facts, tapping her fingers on the desk, listening to the fading sounds of the rush hour outside. The afternoon was becoming evening, and very soon it would start to get dark.

"This man is a local, for sure. And the police might know where he hangs out, locally. He's a trouble causer who's been in prison and now he's been released back into the community. If he's been committing these crimes, Dale will have been around the area, I am sure. They'll know where he's likely to be."

"Let's ask them, then," Owen said.

They stood up and hurried through to the front office.

"You have a past offender, now paroled, name of Dale Crain," May said to the officer at the desk. Immediately she saw recognition in his eyes.

"He's the one who panhandles at the intersection in town, isn't he?"

May felt a flare of hope. Perhaps they would get somewhere now.

"I don't know about that. I know he was arrested and jailed for attacking someone with a hammer two years ago. And that according to the photo in his file, he's blond, five-ten, and thirty-five years old.

"Same guy," the officer said. "Same guy, for sure. He's a nuisance but seems to be a non-violent one since his parole, although if he's a suspect, then maybe not so much. Doesn't much like visitors from out of town, that's for sure. He's been reported a couple of times in the past few weeks for shouting at tour buses, swearing at vacationers, that sort of thing. Nothing that warrants an arrest so far, but we are watching him."

"Where's he likely to be now?" May asked.

The officer checked his watch.

"He won't be at the intersection now. He doesn't stay there after dark. Daylight hours only. I guess he has a room somewhere, but I'm not sure where."

The other officer, working at the back of the lobby, glanced up.

"If that's the blond guy who's at the traffic light sometimes, you could either try the local gym or the local diner. I've seen him in both places in the evenings. He doesn't spend much time in the gym, I think he goes more for the music and the shower. And the diner, for food and a beer."

"Let's try both," May said.

"Be warned, though," the officer said. "He doesn't like the police. Doesn't trust us. If you see him, he's liable to hotfoot it out of wherever he is and disappear."

"Thanks for the warning," Owen said.

Finding Dale Crain was now a priority, but the fact that he was evasive and scared of the police was not going to make the job easy. May knew that they were going to have to use cunning, as well as luck, if they were going to succeed in capturing this strong suspect.

"Shall we try the gym first?" she said to Owen, as they hurried out of the police department.

"Let's do that. I see it's on this same road, all the way down the other end," Owen said, consulting his phone's map.

May got in her car, now feeling very aware of looking like the police. They didn't want to do that. They didn't want to give Dale Crain any kind of a heads-up on who they were.

In the car, she took off her blue jacket and put on a white knit top that she'd left on the back seat a while ago.

"Do you think this looks better?" she asked Owen.

He regarded her solemnly. "I think it looks great on you. But if you're asking whether you look like police, definitely less so than you did. If I were him, I wouldn't be alerted if you arrived looking like that."

"Good. Because I don't want him running away if he sees us," May said.

"Especially when I've got a feeling about this guy," Owen said. "I think his motive for wanting to kill these three tourists is a very strong one. And he has a history of violence. I hope we can get to him before he gets away, because these types of people sometimes seem to have this weird sixth sense about the police."

Sometimes, people ran. Sometimes, people vanished. Sometimes, bad guys could not be found. What Owen was saying was true. They would need luck and good timing to get Dale Crain fast. And fast was the only option they had in these circumstances, with the mayor breathing angrily down their necks.

They headed down the road on the short drive to the gym and climbed out of the car. As she walked up the steps to the small but busy gym, May was keeping the image of Dale's features firmly in her mind: narrow blue eyes, a small mouth, heavy shoulders, and a mop of blond hair—but hair could easily be concealed. It was the other features she needed to keep a lookout for also.

They strolled into the gym, and May quickly detoured to the front desk, hoping to keep her questioning as unobtrusive as possible while she showed her badge, cradled in her palm.

"We're police, seeking a suspect by the name of Dale Crain," she explained. "Do you know if he's here?"

The receptionist shrugged apologetically. "I'm new here. I don't know many of the members by name, but you're welcome to take a look."

"Thank you," May murmured. She headed quickly into the gym, walking casually so as not to arouse suspicion, taking a good look around. Since Dale Crain was not a big user of the gym equipment, she was looking more for the people who were idling, relaxing, going through the motions.

There were quite a few of those, but none who fitted his description.

"Do you want to look in the men's change room?" she asked Owen, who nodded, moving quickly to the door. But a few moments later, he was out again.

"No luck," he said ruefully. "Perhaps he's at the diner?"

"I guess he must be, because he definitely isn't here," May said. Feeling discouraged, she headed out.

"Let's check the diner, at least," Owen said.

But, as they headed down the stairs, May's eyes were caught by a flash of movement, so sudden that she almost missed it.

It looked to her as if someone was about to head into the gym, but at the last moment, had changed their mind and veered out again.

Were Dale's instincts good enough to spot them from such a distance and in casual clothes? She had been walking with Owen though, and with his clean-cut looks and blue jacket, he did give the air of law enforcement. And perhaps Dale was just ultra-suspicious, she wondered.

At any rate, there was only one person that was in sight now, a stocky man of average height, walking briskly down the sidewalk away from the gym.

"Is that him?" May asked.

"It could be," Owen said, narrowing his eyes as he stared into the evening gloom.

Wanting to know and hoping that her idea might get a reaction from him, she began to shout as she power walked behind him, closing the distance as fast as she could.

"Hey! Dale! Dale Crain. Is that you? Stop, please. We need to talk to you."

The man didn't stop. But he began to run.

It was a dead giveaway. This must be Dale, and he was now doing his best to avoid them. And, as he ducked sideways across the street, causing a squeal of brakes and a blare of horns, May realized he might just get his way.

"Stop! Dale Crain, we need to talk to you!" she yelled as loud as she could.

And then, since her words had only made him run faster, May did the only thing left to do.

She sprinted across the street, dodging through the traffic herself, hearing brakes screech and the angry chorus of horns.

It didn't matter. Right now, the only thing that mattered was catching up with this suspect before he proved his ability to vanish into thin air.

CHAPTER FIFTEEN

May pounded after Dale Crain, wishing that it wasn't already getting dark because cover of darkness would make it so much easier for this strong suspect to disappear. Especially as he was fleeing to the easterly side of town, on the downhill slope where the shadows were longer, and it was already almost night.

Owen was racing alongside her, veering to her left as they reached the line of parked cars on the side of the road.

"Stop! Police!" she yelled, but to no avail. In fact, May feared, saying the word 'Police', although necessary for protocol, was making him run faster.

Worse still, his dark clothing made it all but impossible to see him as he dodged away. All she could look out for was the yellow blur of his blond hair as he sped along. Otherwise, he was nothing more than a shadow, now darting beyond the buildings at the end of the road and disappearing into the area beyond.

"He's going to lose us!" she called to Owen. "We need to cut him off!"

"Got you!" Owen yelled back.

May was relieved to see that Owen veered to the left, making a dash for the other side of the building, dodging cars as he went. With any luck, this would prevent Dale from doubling back.

Together, they raced down the sidewalk. May veered around the corner, in pursuit of Dale, and found herself running through a parking lot with a small coffee shop beyond. The place was starting to close, the outdoor chairs were being stacked, and the day's canopies were beginning to be taken down. Dale was ahead of her, running hard. He hadn't doubled back but had other strategies in mind to escape her.

As Dale sprinted past the café, he shoved one of the stacks of chairs, hard. The tall plastic stack swayed and fell, chairs clattering and tumbling onto the sidewalk and into May's path. Waving her arms to keep her balance, she dodged through them, shouting, "Sorry!" to the waitress who was staring at her in consternation from the coffee shop's entrance.

Something else toppled into her path, a folded sun umbrella. May didn't have time to get out of its way, so she jumped wildly over it. She almost fell, stumbling to the sidewalk. But she caught herself and kept running, straining for speed, gasping for breath.

She had to keep this guy in sight. She had to grab him.

Now, he was ahead of her, near the end of the parking lot and he was sprinting across an open area, an expanse of grass that looked to be a large park, leading out to the forested area beyond. And then, there was just the darkness, the blackness of night that would hide Dale completely.

Dale was already making headway through the park, veering toward a dark cluster of trees. She heard his feet, thumping over the grass, seemingly in time with the panicked beats of her own heart.

"He's getting away!" May gasped. She didn't have time to say more. All her energy, all her focus, was on catching up with this fleeing suspect.

The park was dark, but there were streetlights on the sidewalk, as well as lamps in the trees. There was just enough light for her to see the pale shape of his head as he raced into the gloom.

Owen was somewhere nearby, she knew. But she couldn't see where, so right now, she was on her own.

May sprinted along the grass, stumbling over the uneven surface.

She caught herself, righting her balance, and forcing herself to concentrate on where she was going, as well as keep Dale in sight.

The trees ahead were a dark mass, and she tried to focus on him, as he was now even more difficult to see.

"Dale Crain, stop running! We just want to ask you a few questions," she gasped. Her words were ragged, and she wasn't sure her voice carried.

The man ahead of her was racing to the forest at top speed, his dark clothing blending seamlessly with the shadows. He was little more than a shadow himself, making it even more difficult to see him.

She saw the pale blur of his head in the darkness, and then he veered to the right, heading toward a darker patch of trees. It seemed like he knew where he was going, and she feared that he might have a bolt hole in the forest that he was aiming to reach.

Did he? Or was he just a fast runner, choosing the easiest way to get away from her? It definitely seemed like he had a destination in mind, the way he was racing ahead, practically flying over the rough terrain.

She pushed harder, willing herself to speed, doing her utmost to gain on him.

Hope surged through her as she saw Owen power into the open area. He had taken the opposite way and had now burst into the park at an entry point closer to the woods. She turned her head, catching sight of him in the gloom, still running hard. He was closing in on Dale at an angle.

The fugitive flung himself forward, veering away into the trees. The heavy underbrush rustled as he raced into the forest, trying to lose himself among the oaks and pines.

But May could see him now, could follow the path he'd taken, and better still, Owen was catching up. Her partner blasted into the forest from farther along the trail, and with a flash of relief, May realized that between the two of them, they would be able to cut him off.

Dale was now running deeper into the trees, and May could hear him pushing through the brush, his feet pounding over the ground.

She saw the pale flash of his head, his blond hair bouncing as he ran.

May drove herself, racing through the woods now, heading for the spot where Owen was closing in on Dale. If he could just catch up with him, they could grab him. But she could still see that Dale was forcing himself to run faster, driven by a need to escape their presence—and their questions.

The man was grunting with effort, the sound carrying back to May over the rustle of leaves and the swish of branches. But finally, he was tiring. He was slowing with each step. And Owen was now racing up to him on his right, as May gave it one last effort, surging ahead to his left.

He was going to be caught. With a sense of exhausted triumph, she realized they had done it. Their efforts had paid off.

They each grabbed one of the flagging fugitive's arms at the same time.

Dale snarled and struggled but May hung on as tight as she could. After that chase, there was no way she was letting this guy go. Fit as she was, she wasn't sure if she could manage another sprint at that speed, not until she'd had the chance to catch her breath.

"We need to ask you some questions," she panted.

They were miles from the nearest police department, and it was getting late. May made the call that since this suspect was all run out, and they had him firmly contained, it would be better to question him right here.

"I don't want to answer anything. I don't trust the police!" he retorted, breathing so hard his breath was literally wheezing from his lungs.

"If you don't answer, we will take you into the police department and keep you in an interrogation room until you're ready to talk," she threatened him. Even though she'd already decided against this plan, he didn't need to know that.

Those words definitely packed a punch. Dale looked horrified.

"No man! Don't do that. I've spent enough time in police custody! You guys are brutal!"

"We're not being brutal to you. We're seeking information. You're the one making it difficult by running away," May pointed out.

"Well, you started it by chasing me," he retorted.

May was not going to comment on that logic or get caught up in such a pointless argument. Instead, she pushed forward.

"You used to stay in the historic houses near the lake. There have recently been murders in three of those homes. I understand you had big issues with being removed from one of those properties," May said.

"The historic homes?" Was it her imagination or did he look paler.

"Yes. The row of houses down the hill, bordering the river and the lake," May said. "Three of the homes near the bottom of the hill have been targeted."

She saw a flash of recognition in his eyes.

"I didn't stay there. I stayed farther up the road. Not in the houses lower down."

"It's still within the historic area, and close enough for us to be very interested in whether you might have had a motive to 'discourage' other people from living there. Seeing you were very reluctant to be evicted," May said. "Because to me, your motive seems strong. And you have a criminal record. Have you been there since you were paroled?"

"Yes, yes I have."

"Tell me when?" May asked, now feeling hopeful that they were getting somewhere.

Dale was looking less confident now. In fact, he was looking rather hunted.

"Look, okay. You want the truth?"

"Of course," May said, wondering if this meant they would get the truth or just the lie she expected.

But Dale looked very serious as he stepped closer to her.

"I'll tell you the honest truth. But I don't want to be in trouble for it. I know about those houses. And if you want to know, then yes, I'll tell you." He spoke in a low voice, almost a whisper.

May couldn't work out whether she was going to get a confession, or whether Dale was going to give them a new lead. But either way, she couldn't help feeling curious and expectant as she leaned toward him to hear what he was going to say.

CHAPTER SIXTEEN

Dale leaned forward toward May, and she heard him speak again, in a voice so soft it was little more than a whisper.

Her ears were straining, waiting to catch every word. Every syllable. Right now, any information might give them a lead, and although she hoped for a confession, she knew Dale was also very familiar with the area. If he was not the killer, he might have heard or seen something important.

"Those houses, down the bottom, I don't go there, and I would never go inside," he murmured to her. "I used to pass by them, years ago, and that's when I realized that those houses are haunted. Particularly number four Windrush. That's as haunted as you can get."

May's eyes widened. This was not what she'd expected and in fact, not something she'd thought this man would say at all. It hadn't seemed like who he was. She was startled by this.

Number four Windrush was where the writers retreat had been held.

"Haunted?" Owen repeated, surprised.

Now that his inhibitions to speak had been overcome, there was no stopping Dale as he continued. "Everyone who lives nearby, or who has lived there, knows it. I've seen and heard things myself. Weird voices, movements and sounds, lights flickering in empty rooms. Shadows going in and out. If you ask me, it's the ghost that has been doing these killings."

May sighed. She'd just pushed herself to the limits in this frenzied chase, only to discover that this suspect had nothing coherent to say.

"I've been back to that part of town recently since I've been out of prison. As I told you. I love the area, it's like, my heart place, you know? But I don't go down the hill that far. I saw them there, still there, for sure. The house was empty, but it wasn't. Ghosts don't go away. It's haunted, and always will be."

May was wondering if all this talk of ghosts could be a distraction to try and deflect their attention from the fact that he was the killer. If it was, she needed to check his alibi. If not, she needed to figure out if this information was going to be useful or important. Perhaps she could learn something from his local knowledge.

"Where were you earlier this afternoon?" she asked, knowing that the timing of the most recent murder would be the easiest of the three alibis to confirm. His answer surprised her.

"I was at the roadhouse," he said. "As of last week, I have a job there. I wash dishes and clean up the tables there, six days a week, from one p.m. to six-thirty p.m. I can show you my message confirming the employment, and also my timecard. I have it on my phone."

He took his phone out and showed her the texts he'd received for getting the job, and the automatic confirmation texts for clocking in and out of work.

That would have ruled out the time frame for the most recent murder, May knew, and since this was a serial crime, being cleared of one meant being cleared of all. He was not their killer.

Evening was wearing on, her legs were aching, and they were back to the beginning in terms of likely killers. This case was not going well.

"Thanks for the information," May said, now feeling totally discouraged. They went their separate ways, with Dale melting into the forest and May and Owen trudging back to the car.

"You know, I had a thought when Dale was telling us about the hauntings," she said. "Those rentals. Let's look into them more carefully, find out who owns them and who's involved with them. Perhaps we've been missing something there, and what Dale said to us was actually true."

"How do you mean?" Owen asked.

"Perhaps, as a local, Dale noticed activity there. Perhaps one of the people who bought them, or who rents them out, might be involved in something criminal. Maybe because the places can no longer be used for that purpose with all the tourism in the area, one of the owners is angry. They might be hoping to clear them out again, degrade the area, get people to leave, so they can go back to their activities again."

"That might also be why Dale heard noises and saw movement," Owen agreed thoughtfully. "He could have noticed something if the homes are being used to do drug deals, to sell illicit substances, trade in banned items, or used for the prostitution trade. It's a strong possibility."

May was about to expand on this promising direction when her phone started ringing, interrupting her thoughts.

Immediately her pulse sped up, as she worried that a ringing phone could be the news of yet another kill. But when she checked the incoming call, it was from a number she didn't know.

She picked it up as she and Owen trudged across the park, heading back to Cole Hill's main street.

"Deputy Moore speaking," she said.

An officious female voice replied. "Oh, good evening, Deputy. I'm Di Wolfe, calling from the mayor's office."

"From the mayor's office?" May repeated, worried now.

"That's right. We're organizing a press conference with the mayor's secretary and a few other movers and shakers from the town. We've got a representative from the tourism board, the school principal, three hotel owners, and a couple of other business owners. And we'd like a police representative there to answer any questions. So, if you could please organize somebody to attend?"

"Where and when is this?" May asked.

"We're kicking off in twenty minutes," the woman told her with gleeful satisfaction, as May gasped. "And it's at the Cole Hill town hall."

"Twenty minutes?" May said incredulously. She was feeling frustrated and angry with the mayor, but she could not defy his orders. That would put her job on the line.

"That's correct. I look forward to meeting whoever you send. Do make sure they're up to date on the case. It'll probably take a couple of hours."

She disconnected just as May was saying, "But—"

"Well!" she said, feeling as if this was just one problem too many in this stressful day.

"Did I hear right? They want one of us at some sort of press conference now?" Owen said.

"That's correct. You heard right," May said, feeling stressed to the nines that this power struggle was still going on. Surely the mayor should have realized that the police were not personal employees to be at his beck and call, but independent, unbiased law enforcement officials who were dedicating every moment to this challenging case.

"Is the mayor going to be there?" Owen asked.

"It didn't sound like it. His secretary is there," May said.

"So, this whole thing is like a bullying tactic. That's what it feels like to me," Owen said angrily. "They're now putting the pressure on by forcing us to be at their beck and call, when what we should really be doing is focusing on the case!"

"But we can't refuse," May said, feeling frustrated. "Mayor Tillman will be really angry if we do, and then he'll take it out on Sheriff Jack, and the whole Fairshore police department will suffer."

"You're right. We can't say no to it. But May, I'll go. It's going to be a stupid waste of time, but at least I'm up to date on the case. I know what to say and what not to say. This will be a good chance to get the public on our side, and I can put the word out that we need information and leads. So, it might have a positive outcome, and it'll free you up to continue."

May felt huge relief that she had such a supportive deputy. And Owen was good with the press and did know what to say and how to say it. He was very diplomatic, in fact. She knew she could trust Owen. She knew he'd do well.

She felt grateful that he was going to be able to attend that press conference and take the pressure off her.

It was going to be a long night of chasing leads, even though she knew it was the only way to solve this crime. The break in this case, the real clue that would lead to the killer, must surely be somewhere right in front of her.

"Thank you, Owen. It's a spoke in our wheel, but if you can go, it'll be best. I'll drop you off there now, on the way back to the police department, and then you can just walk to the police department when you're done. It's just a couple of blocks from the town hall, and if I've gone somewhere else, you can sign out a car and meet me."

"That'll work, and I'll be glad to handle it." Owen sounded ready for the challenge.

They would now be going their separate ways. She'd be without her partner thanks to the mayor's interference. The mayor's agenda wasn't going to include May's safety.

She felt a pang of fear. This was a killer she was chasing, and a brutal killer at that.

And if there were illicit activities taking place in those old houses, May knew this could end up being a dangerous part of the investigation. Now, because of the new circumstances, she would be going at it alone.

CHAPTER SEVENTEEN

After dropping Owen at the Cole Hill town hall for the press conference that May was still seething about, she headed down the road to the police department to get started on the first step of her research. She felt motivated at the thought of looking into the ownership of these affected properties, and the ones nearby. May hoped that the next hour would give her some insight into the owners themselves and their possible illegal activities.

If she found out anything, May knew she was going to have to head straight out to investigate it, with or without Owen by her side. And she very much doubted this press conference would wrap up any time soon. She was sure it would take at least a couple of hours.

But she couldn't delay. Calling out a quick greeting to the officer at the front desk, May rushed through to the back office.

There, she got out her laptop and opened it up, navigating her way to the set of records she needed. Who owned these homes and who rented them out?

May hoped this information would give her some important insight.

As she scrolled through the records, jotting down notes and pasting information, she realized she was starting to see a pattern here.

Of the four properties right at the bottom of the hill, two were owned by an investor called Ian Arnott, who rented them out to vacationers and for events.

And the two on either side of those were owned by a different company, Dolphin Management, which was owned by a man called Patrick Callaway.

And he, too, rented them out for vacations and events.

The third property, which had been affected by the most recent murder, was owned by a big conglomerate that didn't own any other property in that area, but it was bordered by properties owned by each of these two local men. It seemed like their names were coming up a lot, May realized.

She began by looking back at the records for the previous years, trying to create a time frame for when the two men had bought the properties. Interestingly, it seemed that both properties had been acquired by their new owners about a year ago. There had been a rush to purchase properties, with many sales occurring at that time. It seemed there had been a mini war in seeking to acquire real estate. May noticed that Callaway had acquired several properties in the same area, although Arnott only owned three.

A significant time frame, she thought. So, these were both fairly new acquisitions. Perhaps that meant something.

May quickly checked to see if either man had a record. Neither did. They seemed to be fine, upstanding, solid citizens. But she was not convinced and wanted to push on and find out more.

Perhaps local news articles could give her more of a background on these two, she hoped. She had a hunch about the two men. She needed to check as thoroughly as she could because missing a detail might mean overlooking the real killer.

With her notes and information displayed in front of her in neat columns, May opened a new window and began some online research to start looking into local news stories on these two property owners, to get a feel for who they were and how they fitted into the area. Perhaps they had some business connections that would prove to be unsavory or borderline illegal.

There were a number of newspaper articles, local news reports and blogs, as well as opinion pieces. May searched through the archives and headlines, looking for anything that might offer her more information.

And there, at last, she found the spark that could have started a raging fire of conflict that ended in the murders.

Riveted by what she was reading, May learned that there had been constant conflict between the two men ever since the properties had been purchased.

Ian Arnott, who owned the center properties, had immediately begun disputing boundaries, requesting a review of the entire properties' layouts. Patrick Callaway had responded with threats and litigation.

Litigation that had paid off. It had cost him a fortune, but Patrick Callaway had been able to successfully prove that the boundaries of his properties actually ran further back than Ian Arnott had first claimed.

As a result, the renovations that Ian Arnott had been planning to do on both his properties had now been scrapped, and Ian Arnott was furious.

The ongoing disputes between the two men had taken several nasty turns and ended in a few other lawsuits which they'd settled out of court. But the conflict had continued, and there were even more reports.

Recently, there was a story about an unlicensed event taking place at the Arnott property, which Patrick Callaway had helpfully reported to the authorities.

"How kind of him," May murmured, fascinated by what she was learning.

The local news outlets had covered the vendetta between the two men extensively, and Patrick Callaway had been a frequent commentator, airing his opinion on the subject of the legal disagreement and the purchase of the properties.

According to these comments he had been polite and calm and had acted with a highly professional approach, as if it were just another matter of business and not something that was obviously very personal.

But Ian Arnott had been the opposite. He'd responded with threats of violence, promises that he would "get even," and had then begun lurking around the Callaway properties, prompting Callaway to get the police to remove him, although no charges had been pressed.

But this was a serious, bitter, and ongoing war between these two rival landowners, May realized. She kept at it, keeping her fingers on the keyboard and her eyes on the screen, while she continued to search through the local news archives, looking for the latest coverage of the ongoing feud.

She found that it showed no signs of abating. Both men had been very public in their comments and had gotten huge airtime. But May had now seen how enmeshed these two men were in this bitter feud, and she realized that it could easily have ended in bloodshed.

May had a strong hunch that one of these men was the killer. Whichever one it was, there was plenty of motive and opportunity. They both most likely believed they had good reason to lash out at the other in the deadliest way possible.

May had to admit, she wasn't ready to dismiss Callaway as a suspect. He had a temper, he had access to a property, and he was in a dispute with the victim.

But her first suspect, the stronger one, was undoubtedly Ian Arnott. Of the two, he seemed more threatening, more prone to violence, and more of an unstable character than Callaway. If she was looking to profile a killer, May was sure that she would come up with a personality very close to the unpleasant characteristics that Arnott was displaying.

And, from the reports, it seemed clear that he'd also had opportunity, being on site and causing trouble a lot of the time.

Incidentally, it seemed things had calmed down in the last couple of weeks, and May wondered if this was because Arnott might have been focusing all his attention on planning the murders.

Whose properties had the killer struck, she wondered. She thought she knew, but she wanted to double check to be sure of the theory that was now starting to make sense.

May turned to her map for the next step of the puzzle she was now piecing together with determination.

"This is correct. I was right," she muttered to herself with a shiver as she mapped them out. The maps told the full story. So far, these murders had taken place on two Callaway properties and one property neighboring a Callaway-owned mansion.

Yet, the Arnott-owned properties were untouched, and that was highly significant to May. Why hadn't Arnott's properties been affected or touched? They were in exactly the same location and yet that duo of stands had been skipped over.

Was Arnott so embroiled in this conflict that he was committing murders that would bring down the value of the entire neighborhood, just to ensure his rival's properties were the most affected? She guessed a wealthy psychopath might not care about that if he was focused only on his goal.

Killing for revenge was a chilling thought, and she knew she needed to get face-to-face with this aggressive landowner as soon as she could, to see if what she feared was true.

There was an after-hours number on his property website and May dialed it quickly, hoping that she could learn the whereabouts of Arnott and confront him tonight.

CHAPTER EIGHTEEN

Kate Toms stared dubiously at the home in front of her.

Though large and imposing, the house was dilapidated, almost threatening, and framed darkly by the setting sun. It was definitely a spooky place, but she put her misgivings firmly aside. This was not the time to complain. She'd been working for the estate agency for just two months and needed to give this exciting new job her all.

Her reason for being here today was to photograph it and then market it to its full potential for an urgent sale. Kate wasn't sure why this owner was selling in such a rush, but she thought it was because a spate of murders had occurred in the properties across the river. This owner wanted this house gone, and it would definitely be better to try and sell it before the murders hit the national news.

Murders aside, she was still keen to market it quickly. Summer was nearly over, but there was still a chance for a quick seasonal sale. At least this was across the river from where the trouble had happened and could be said to be in a different part of the historic district.

Kate wasn't one for doubts, although she did find them thronging her mind as she stared at its looming frontage. If only this owner had put more effort into maintaining the place. It was very run down, despite having a gorgeous view over the park and the lake as well as backing onto the river.

But optimistic as always, pushing back her brown hair and whistling a tune to herself, she decided that the key word here would be "potential." And now she was looking at it in this way, she could see there was tons of potential in this beautiful, spacious home.

This was an older home, a classic piece of architecture, although it had suffered years of neglect.

She knew she would have to be professional, and she would have to keep her wits about her when taking the photos and writing the copy. It needed a lot more work to make it as desirable as it might be, so Kate was planning to put her own spin on the property by taking the best possible photos that enhanced its marketable features.

She was a fast learner when it came to selling homes, and she had picked up that creating the right atmosphere, making the property stand out and feel unique, made people more eager to buy.

"You can do this," she told herself. "Get over yourself."

As she approached the front door, Kate was struck by a strange, unfamiliar sensation. She tried to scold herself, thinking that she'd been viewing too many Halloween movies. But she could not help it, she felt a tension in the air, a sense of foreboding, as she put her hand on the door, took out the key, unlocked it, and opened it.

The door swung open with surprising ease considering the state of the property. Kate stepped into the hallway, which was littered with clutter, old boxes, ancient coat stands, and broken tiles. But the rooms beyond looked clearer. Her eyes swept the area, looking for the best shots and mentally setting them up in her mind, which was the best way to shoot in these situations, especially given the darkening light. Her camera had a good flash on it which would help.

She noted the staircase and the imposing archway that led to an old lounge and decided to start with these.

Putting down her purse, she quickly set up her tripod and readied the camera, framing the shot. This was the first step, choosing the right angle and the right kind of view. As a professional, she knew how important it was to get the best possible shot of the property. It was all about the first impressions. There was a dramatic shape to the archway that was really beautiful.

Kate was about to take the shot when she heard a noise. She looked up, frowning, and stared down the dark hallway. It hadn't been a loud noise. It had been soft, almost furtive. Rats? But she'd been in old homes with rats before and they had not sounded like this.

Even though she strained her eyes, she could see nothing, and she dismissed the thought. She was sure she was just being paranoid. Usually, she would have asked her fiancé to come along with her to these evening shoots, but he was out of town at a sales conference tonight.

But she knew he would have been a little anxious about her being alone. She was too, but that was just the way of the business. It was very often a case of her being by herself.

She was still thinking about this when she heard a pitter-patter, soft and quiet, again.

Kate turned to the noise and stared down the hallway with a little frown. "Hey?" she called out, looking closer. "Is anyone there?"

There was no answer, and she dismissed it. There could be nobody in this old house, there was nothing to steal, and nobody knew she was going to be here. It had been a last-minute decision to come this way, thinking that the sunset would provide atmospheric lighting.

Anyhow, she was being paid to get the best possible photos, and she was here to do a job, and so far, she hadn't been doing anything except getting distracted. She needed to pull herself back toward herself and focus.

She readied herself for the shot, holding her breath for a moment, and then she clicked the shutter.

It was beautiful. Oozing with atmosphere. It looked almost medieval, and the gracious and spacious room beyond showed just enough detail to fire up a buyer's imagination.

She let out a pleased sigh, moving into the lounge for another shot.

And then, she heard a noise from the upstairs landing, a soft echoing thud, like something had fallen over.

Kate told herself that it was just her imagination working overtime. Probably a bird, landing heavily on the roof. But still, she found her eyes straying to the stairs again.

"Foolish," she scolded herself. "You need to stop feeling nervous about this place. It's not going to hurt you. It's not a house of horrors."

She laughed aloud and then began to take the shot, which was perfect. It showcased the archway and the staircase perfectly in the frame.

She closed her eyes as she took the shot and imagined the new owner taking in the house and falling in love with it.

Looking at the photo, she smiled. That was better. Now she was in her element. She felt confident enough to proceed, taking a shot of the living room and the rooms beyond, and then going upstairs, where she was sure there would be some amazing sunset views that would appeal to an owner's aspirations.

Also, upstairs felt somehow safer, probably because the evening sun would be glowing in through those big southwest-facing windows.

Not that she was scared, just cautious, always cautious and professional.

But she needed to take one more shot in this downstairs area because a viewer would want to see all the rooms, and there were a few more here. The problem is that they were in a really dark area of the house. Luckily, she had a spotlight with her that she could set up that would ensure a highly atmospheric and beautiful photo.

She stepped through into the darker rooms beyond, whistling to herself to calm her nerves, stumbling as her foot hit a piece of wood on the dusty floor.

"Just a few more and we're done!" she soothed herself. "Just a few more pics!"

That's when she heard it, as if her voice had alerted the trouble, coming from behind her, from the hallway. It wasn't coming from inside at all. This was coming from outside, and Kate realized with a rush of fear that someone had opened the front door and come in behind her. She heard the front door slam and the unmistakable sound of a key turning in the lock.

A crunching sound. A footstep. And then a heavy, menacing breath. Finally, a shadow darkened the lounge doorway.

Kate drew in a shaking, terrified gasp.

Her heart hammered in her chest and adrenaline throbbed in her veins, seeming to make time slow down, as if every second mattered in the brief window she had to make a decision.

In that moment, Kate decided to trust her instincts.

A normal person would have called out, yelled a greeting, or knocked. None of that had happened. She wasn't going to wait around. Not when murders had happened in nearby properties. Murders!

In a panic, Kate fled.

She ran through the house, glancing around her in desperation, wondering where she could hide, how she could get away, until she could call for help. She could call her fiancé, get him to call the police, get someone here to help her.

Her stomach felt lodged in her throat. It was as if she was running through a terrible dream. Somehow none of this felt real.

Down here, perhaps. This staircase seemed to lead down to the basement and she remembered, vaguely, the owner telling her it was a room that was lockable.

She stumbled down the staircase to the dark, narrow doorway below, breathing in dust and damp and the feeling of age and decay.

There was a key in the door. With a feeling of utter relief, she grabbed it, tugged the door open, slammed it behind her, and fumbled in the now total darkness.

She found the lock and twisted the key. She was safe, locked in and locked away. Kate let out a deep breath that was not relief because she knew she was still in danger. Rather, it was that she'd had a stay of execution and now she had a chance.

She took out her phone with quivering hands and its screen provided a small pool of light in this dusty room.

But when Kate tried to make the call, she realized to her horror that there was no signal in this underground, windowless room. The call would not connect. She tried again, with the same result.

She couldn't call for help. She had no means of communicating with the outside world.

And then, from upstairs, she heard slow, deliberate footsteps, making their way heavily down toward the basement door.

CHAPTER NINETEEN

May dialed the after-hours number for Arnott Properties, hoping that whoever picked up would know where Ian Arnott was and be able to send her his way. Based on the amount of bad blood between these two property owners, she was very interested in speaking to him and fast.

There was so much at stake for Arnott, after all: financial gain, property interests, but above and beyond that, a serious vendetta in which hatred and ego were fueling the flames between the two rivals.

Arnott was definitely the one who had escalated the conflict. The kills had occurred on two Callaway-owned properties and one property that neighbored a Callaway home. But May knew that once psychopathic killings started, the original motives might become blurred and the need to kill could take over.

From the written words and also the unspoken slants of the pieces she had read, she understood that Arnott was a man with a serious aggressive streak and a ruthless side to him.

Although Kerry was the hotshot FBI profiler, May knew a thing or two about human nature. This could easily fit the description of a serial killer.

A man angry at the world, angry at his colleagues, angry at his rivals, and one who would feel justified in using violence to bring things in his favor.

Finally, the call connected, and a woman picked up.

"Arnott Properties, can I help?" she asked, sounding stressed.

"I'm looking for Ian Arnott, please," May said.

The woman hesitated. "He's not here right now," she said cautiously. "This is an after-hours number to help with inquiries on our properties."

May had the uneasy feeling that she'd be more likely to get ahold of Ian if she said she was a prospective buyer with millions to spend. But she couldn't tell such a whopping lie. In fact, she couldn't tell any lies at all. She was bound by her ethics as a police officer to tell the truth.

"I'm Deputy May Moore, and I'm investigating a serial murder case in properties adjacent to some of the homes that Ian Arnott owns," she said, hearing the woman's gasp.

"What?" The woman sounded shocked. "The murders?"

"I'm looking for Ian Arnott to ask him some questions, and it's really important that I speak to him. Where is he?

"I'm sorry," the woman said. "I can't call him. I…er…I don't have his contact details."

"You don't have his emergency contact details?" May asked. She didn't bother to hide how incredulous she sounded at this obvious lie.

"No," the woman said, sounding more and more uncomfortable.

"Why not?" May asked, frowning.

"He's...he's a private individual," the woman said. "He likes his boundaries."

"Well, I'm a police officer, and I'm investigating a murder case," May said. She decided it was time to up the ante. This woman wasn't responding to being asked nicely, so May was going to make sure to point out the level of inconvenience that could come her way if she didn't spill the information.

She was hoping that if she did this, it would pressure this woman to the point of giving up the details that May was totally sure she possessed.

"If you can't give me his contact details, that's alright," she then said.

"Oh, good," the woman said, sounding relieved. Too soon, as it happened. May plowed forward inexorably.

"However, seeing that we do need to speak to a representative from Arnott Properties tonight, I'm going to need you to come to the Cole Hill police department immediately for questioning. Either you can drive here right now, or I will come and pick you up. Which will work better for you, ma'am?" May asked, making sure to sound helpful.

There was a horrified pause. Clearly, this was a worst-case scenario come to life, and the woman was now panicking.

"Look, I can't give you Mr. Arnott's number, but I can tell you where he is," she said breathlessly. "I have his diary on my computer. Will that work for you?"

"You're going to give me his address?" May asked.

"No, no. He's not at home this evening. He's currently attending a function at Three Trees Lodge. It's a fundraiser evening hosted by the mayor and some of the area's leading businessmen. They're raising money for the new wing at the children's hospital," the woman said. "I'm sure he'd be happy to speak with you while he's there if it's so urgent. Will that work for you?"

While being thrilled that she had the information she needed, May felt blindsided by the bombshell this woman had unleashed on her.

Mr. Arnott was at a function hosted by the mayor?

Did the mayor have any idea that, while flinging every level of criticism at the local police, he most likely had the killer sitting at one of his own function tables?

She felt shocked by this information.

"Thank you. Yes, that will be acceptable," she told the woman, who immediately hung up after saying a relieved goodbye.

That left May considering her options big-time.

If Arnott wasn't such a strong suspect, she'd have rethought the idea. Going into a function held by the mayor and dragging one of his own VIP guests out for questioning was not going to be well-received. In fact, May was sure that Mayor Tillman would be absolutely furious. He would consider it interference and would take it personally. May had no doubt that a man like him would not think it possible that he could consort with killers. His own ego and self-belief wouldn't allow him to entertain such an idea.

He would be outraged, and May would be in the firing line. Her job, her role as a police officer—everything she had worked for—would be even more at risk than it already was.

How she wished this could wait till tomorrow.

But at the same time, if she didn't do this, she would be letting down the victims themselves, their grieving families, and all the people in town who would remain in danger. What if Arnott left the function and went straight to the historic district to kill again?

Given all of that, there was no way she could delay. Not when there were so many murders being committed in such a frighteningly short time frame. She had to prevent any further loss of life, and do whatever it took, even if that meant ruining an entire official function with her surprise arrival.

She had a moral obligation to do this. She couldn't walk away from a chance to catch a murderer. And she wasn't going to let that opportunity pass. Not when all the other leads had vanished into thin air.

This was the best lead she had so far, and she needed to follow it up, despite the political fallout that would happen if she didn't play her cards very, very carefully.

Never had she thought that she would be heading straight into such a minefield, though. May got to her feet, feeling slightly sick to her stomach.

I'm not going to think about the consequences, she told herself. *I just have to do this.*

With a sense of grim determination, May grabbed her jacket and purse and headed out of the police department. She was hell bent on getting to Three Trees Lodge as fast as she could to confront the suspected killer, who also happened to be a political associate of the town mayor.

CHAPTER TWENTY

The man who spoke to the dead was frantic.

He'd arrived at his destination, but it was silent and dark. This was the place he'd heard from all the way across the river. It was as if razors had been cutting into his head, hearing their shouts and music and laughter, as well as the incessant yapping of a dog.

He'd tried to shut it out and communicate with the dead, but they had sulkily refused to say a word. They were angry now, he realized. The dead were mad at him because he wasn't doing enough. And the problem had been clear, it was the noisy house on the other side of the river. That was the one he needed to silence. He needed to go in there, urgently, and kill. But now that he was here, the house was silent. Locked up tight. The people making the noise had gone.

But the spirits hadn't forgiven him. He couldn't hear their voices anymore.

Not the old woman, whose cackling tones sounded a little like a faint flock of geese.

Not the strange man whose voice was like the harsh, wailing moan of wind in the trees.

And not the other voice, the ageless one, that was little more than a sigh and that he could only hear when things were very quiet. He knew this must be an old, tired spirit. He couldn't understand its words, but still, it deserved to be heard.

Rage surged through him once again, the feeling intense and red-hot. It sparked him into action, and he knew the time had come to do what he needed to do, once again.

He should have come here immediately, but he'd thought that he could take his time, plan, and even wait until darkness fell, so it would be easier to do his work. So, instead of rushing out, he'd thoughtfully enjoyed the preparation time. And it had backfired on him. By the time he'd gotten himself ready, clothed himself, and waited for the afternoon traffic to die down so that it was quiet enough for him to think clearly, he had been too late.

The house was all closed up. The door was locked, the windows were dark, and it was totally quiet. He could tell nobody was here, nobody at all. And these were vacation rentals. These terrible people and their noise might have gone for the evening or else checked out for good. He had no way of knowing, and he couldn't even peek through a window to see if anyone was there—the way he'd done for his previous target—because the curtains were all closed.

But he needed to kill. The voices were telling him, imploring him to kill. Now it was the only thing they were saying, and finally, he understood their message clearly.

The house was empty, but with his sensitive hearing, he picked up sounds in the house next door.

There was a faint light inside and a car outside. A person was here, probably only one person.

Now starting to grin with excitement and anticipation, he moved toward this old, derelict home.

He could tell the intruder was alone. He could hear only one set of footsteps, but this person was trampling through the property like he or she owned the place. A woman's footsteps, he realized, listening again.

A chill went through him. What if she did own the place? What if she was the new owner, who was going to rip and demolish, hammer and bang, drowning out these voices for months while she "renovated" their space?

Why was she here if she wasn't the owner?

He didn't know. But he knew now that, with the other house empty, she was now the enemy. He had to protect the spirits, who spoke to him and who were all here because they needed him to listen.

He didn't want to hurt her, but if he had to, he would.

Prickling with adrenaline and shaking with rage, he moved to the side window and listened.

He breathed in, then out, breathing slowly. He needed to be calm, controlled, and cold.

There was only one way to do this, and he knew he would have to be quick and brutal with it. He would have to silence her the way he had quieted down the others, using his weapon. He had it with him. It would be easy to do.

He opened the door and walked inside, closing and locking it behind him so she couldn't get out again. As he paced through the house softly, he heard the click of a shutter and realized she was taking photos. So, she must be "marketing" it. Yes, he knew what that would mean. It would mean ranks of people swarming in here at all hours, looking at it and considering whether to buy it or not. He could imagine their sharp, harsh voices. They would bring their kids, and the kids would scream and run around, their footsteps battering on the tiles.

They would bring their phones, which would buzz, trill, and beep. They might even bring pets, like the dogs he could still remember barking and yapping when he tried to sleep. They might play music, a sound he hated, and was sure the spirits did too.

He had to protect the home.

He couldn't let them in here. Not if he wanted to hear the voices.

He understood now that he needed to act fast. This was nothing short of an emergency. It signaled potential disaster for him.

The killing was just a means to an end. He had to protect the house and the spirits. He would not allow them to be crushed and drowned out, to suffer the noise.

He crept forward.

She was in the dining room, her back to him, a light shining onto the majestic room. He could see her through the partly open door.

Moving forward eagerly, he sighed as he thought about the satisfaction he would gain from doing this important work.

But, to his horror, he sighed too loud.

He had made a terrible error. He had been noisy enough for her to hear, and so she did. She heard. Her indrawn gasp gave it away. And then with a clatter of footsteps, she fled.

He froze, not believing what was happening, feeling a rush of guilt that now her pounding feet were disturbing the spirits and that he himself was the one who had caused this.

He clutched his weapon in hands that felt suddenly damp and cold. Her footsteps stormed down the stairs. She was fleeing. She must know about the basement room.

And a chill shuddered through him as he heard her fumbling with the key, slamming the door, and then locking it behind her.

She'd locked herself in! He could not believe the extent of this catastrophe. It had to be stopped. Somehow, he now had to manage this terrible scenario that he himself had caused.

The man who spoke to the dead paced down the stairs, trying to walk softly in apology to the spirits.

He heard her breath, fast and terrified. She knew he was coming. Perhaps he could reason with her.

"Let me in," he whispered. It felt strange to speak to another person in this sacred place. Normally, he only listened to the faint sounds of the spirits.

Her breath caught in a sob of fear.

"Let me in," he pleaded, his voice harsh, even though he was trying for a wheedling note. He gripped the door handle and tried to turn it, rattling it, and heard her cry of fear. It ripped through his ears like a blade, sharp and disruptive.

She was desperate now, he could tell. He heard her scrambling around, shoving things. She was screaming, yelling for help, and the noise was driving him to the brink of insanity.

"Shut up!" he hissed, but she wasn't listening to him. She screamed louder.

"Help me! Someone! Help me!" she cried.

His breath hissed out of his throat. There was no way she was going to let him in and no way she was going to stop shouting. What if this hideous noise put the spirits off so badly that they were silenced forever? That was a terrible thought, and he was not going to allow it to happen.

He tried to calm himself, but he was too full of rage, too frantic about what she was doing. There was only one answer, he realized. Only one thing he could do. It would also create noise, but if he did it right, the noise would be quick, and it would last for a short time only. The spirits would forgive him because he was doing it for them.

And when he'd done it, all would be quiet again.

His chest heaving, but now grinning in satisfaction, the man turned away and paced through the house, looking for the right weapon that would allow him to break through the door and get to her.

There was nothing here he could use, but he remembered that he'd seen something in one of the other homes, back on the far side of the river. It was a large steel bar, rusted but heavy and strong. He hoped this would work. But if it didn't, he had thought of a plan B, and he'd bring the equipment for that too. He could easily make sure his victim would be too terrified to leave.

"I'm waiting for you here," he screamed in the direction of the basement, just to make sure she stayed put. "Come out, any time. I'm ready, darling! Ready for you!"

Then, seething inwardly with rage, he forced himself to walk quietly out of the house to go and find what he needed.

CHAPTER TWENTY ONE

On the way to the mayor's function, May felt very alone. She was going into this single-handed and she knew it was going to be highly risky. Her job was on the line. Her career and her future were at stake. She was actually going to go in and gate-crash the mayor's own fundraiser in her efforts to solve this crime and arrest the right suspect.

With Owen at the press conference, she had no partner. No backup.

And worryingly, she'd also not managed to pick up anything of real substance so far on Ian Arnott. May was convinced there must be something. But she hadn't been able to find anything that directly linked him to criminal activities. Having such information would smooth the way when she got to Three Trees Lodge. The mayor could argue a future theory but not a past record.

Suddenly, a thought occurred to her. She knew someone who could help. If there was information to be discovered, she had the connection in high places who could dig it up.

May got on the phone and called Kerry, hoping that her sister would pick up. It was nearly eight p.m. but that didn't mean she wouldn't still be in a meeting, or else in a helicopter, or else taking down a drug lord or criminal kingpin.

But she was in luck as Kerry answered on the third ring.

"May," she said. She didn't sound too pleased, and a moment later, May found out why. "Is this about this video of Lauren? Because if so, you need to give me more time. It takes hours to go through all the old footage to look for a dead pixel. I'm a busy law enforcement officer, you know! I only just got home now! Don't harass me, okay?"

Hastily, May interrupted her.

"No, Kerry. It's not about the video."

"Oh." Kerry sounded deflated now, as if she'd prepared a whole lot more to say and now wasn't going to have the chance to say it. "Oh. Okay. So, what is it about then?"

"I'm heading into a difficult situation."

"What?" Now her sister sounded intrigued.

"I'm going to question a suspect called Ian Arnott. He owns properties in the historic area of Cole Hill, close to where a series of murders have occurred."

"I've heard about those murders," Kerry said, sounding thoughtful now. "Your boss gave us the heads-up this afternoon. He says that if it's not solved by tomorrow morning then he's calling us in to help. Mom's already called me, asking what I want for dinner tomorrow night."

May felt a stab of unease at this news. Even though it was the right thing to do, and Jack had no other choice, she was sure that bringing in the FBI would simply prove to Mayor Tillman that local law enforcement was incompetent. It would be the final nail in her own coffin. It made it all the more imperative to solve this tonight. Especially since the man she needed might, right now, be cozying up to the mayor over fine wine and canapes.

"Ian Arnott has a feud with a neighboring property owner, who owns two of the homes where murders have occurred. He's threatened and bullied. He litigates at the drop of a hat. He's acted in a way that makes me very suspicious of him. He could easily escalate. He's the kind of person who should have been in trouble, but I can't find anything on him."

"Yes, it's often those people who are very quick to threaten and litigate that have their own skeletons concealed," Kerry agreed. "As a profiler, I can confirm that's true."

May felt pleased that even though she was not a qualified FBI profiler, she'd thought the same way.

"So, you want me to see if I can find anything on him?" Kerry asked.

"Yes. It would be so helpful if you could do that. Because the Cole Hill mayor is now making our lives miserable by pressuring us to solve this crime, and Ian Arnott is currently at a fundraiser being held by the mayor. That is literally where I'm headed now."

May could hear how her own voice was shaking. This really was going to be super scary.

Kerry sounded amused and impressed.

"Sis, you're heading for an explosion!"

"And I'm going to be the one lighting the fuse," May admitted.

"Okay, I'll see what I can find, and call you as soon as I know anything. I'll get onto it now."

May felt grateful beyond words to have Kerry in her corner. She'd not been able to pick up anything on Arnott, but that didn't mean he had a clean slate, it just meant that he was a very sly man who might have committed misdemeanors out of state. Kerry could take this further.

"Thanks so much," she said.

She cut the call and gripped the wheel as she headed out to Three Trees Lodge, following the signage that directed her out of town and into an attractive, hilly area near the far side of the lake, beyond the town.

"I can do this," she muttered to herself. "I can do this."

But she had never felt more scared as she approached the imposing lodge. It was clearly a highly expensive and up-market place, nestled into the hillside, with a sloping roof and a glass and timber frontage. Through the glass, May could see the twinkle of chandeliers. In the perfectly paved parking area, a host of luxury vehicles gleamed in the outside lights.

May added her very dusty ride to the row, noticing how her car immediately lowered the tone. Well, she had no illusions that she herself was about to do the same.

She would have to try to be subtle, she decided. Going in with guns blazing, so to speak, would make Mayor Tillman furious. He'd be looking to get payback, and she'd have made a lasting enemy. She needed to enter discreetly, ask for Ian Arnott, and quietly take him aside. She desperately needed not to cause any fuss or draw any attention to herself. This had to be done in a low-key way, she decided.

May could hear the strains of stringed instruments and the chatter of voices. Through the glass, she could see waiters moving between the assembled guests, carrying plates of food, bottles of wine, champagne glasses, and silver trays of hors d'oeuvres.

Mayor Tillman was standing on a dais, and May thought he looked to have just given an opening speech, as there was a smattering of applause.

Clearly, there was going to be some entertainment, because outside the lodge door, May saw a heavily made-up blond-haired woman in a glittering evening dress was waiting, holding a mike in her hand. She must be about to go in and provide live entertainment, which suited her perfectly. With that on the go, it should be no problem to quietly filter through the crowds and find Arnott.

"Excuse me," May said. "Please, wait a moment. I just need to go in."

She wanted to melt into the crowds before this blond made her appearance. Then, when the singing started, it should be easy to do what she needed to.

The blond singer gave her a surprised stare.

"But—" she said.

"It's police business," May told her patiently. "I do need to go in."

For a moment she didn't think she was going to move aside for her, as she walked into the lobby, but she then shuffled over grudgingly, teetering on her heels.

Mayor Tillman was speaking again. She barely heard his words as she walked toward the big, arched doorway leading into the function room, where she saw a red carpet had been placed.

"And now, ladies and gentlemen, it is my pleasure and honor to introduce tonight's entertainment!" the mayor was bellowing into the mike, but May was so preoccupied that she wasn't really listening as she headed determinedly to the door.

"I'd like you to welcome some of the biggest homegrown talent we have in this town! One of our most impressive rising stars, someone who has captured my heart from the first moment I met her and heard her voice. She enthralled me, just as I know she'll enthrall you too. Ladies and gentlemen, I'd like you all to welcome the extremely talented soprano, hailing from Cole Hill itself. Welcome the golden voiced Lillian Graham, who will now be setting the stage alight!"

May stepped onto the red carpet and as she did so, music boomed out, the lights were dimmed, and a spotlight shone directly down on her, blinding her in its light so that she threw up a defensive hand to shield her eyes. Only then did she realize, too late, what the mayor had been saying.

May felt herself turn as red as the carpet. She felt pinned by the spotlight, with no idea what to do in this appalling scenario. For a few moments, the entire scene seemed frozen in time.

Then the music stopped, highlighting the astounded hush that had filled the room. The spotlight turned off and the lights turned back on.

Everyone was looking at May, and she now heard the murmurs of surprised conversation start up from round about.

Too late, with a sense of utter catastrophe, she realized she could not have timed this worse. She'd unintentionally walked in at the wrong moment and had made the biggest possible statement entrance, while also ruining the big reveal of this fundraiser.

As her eyes recovered from the assault of the spotlight, she saw Mayor Tillman on stage.

He was glaring at her with nothing short of murder in his eyes.

CHAPTER TWENTY TWO

The mayor paced toward May with a deadly gleam in his eyes. From the crowds, she heard a few bursts of surprised laughter. One person started slow-clapping. There was even a whistle from somewhere in this well-heeled throng.

Feeling she should offer some sort of apology in the lead-up to her confrontation, May turned to the crowds on each side of the red carpet.

"Sorry," she said. "So sorry. I didn't mean to interrupt. I'm just investigating a case."

"Is this a comedy slot?" some smartass called out.

Trying to ignore him, May began pacing up the red carpet toward Mayor Tillman, who was storming down. They met in the middle.

"What the hell are you doing here?" he spat out.

"Mayor Tillman," she said. "I'm very sorry about this. But I just need to have a quick word with one of your guests—"

"This is deliberate, isn't it?" he snapped. He had an outraged expression on his face, and his fists were clenched, as though he wanted to punch her. The nearby guests were listening interestedly to this exchange. Someone had even started filming it, she saw.

"I just wanted to—"

"You are making a total fool of me," he barked. This is a private event, and the police have no place here."

At that moment a forty-something-year-old woman in a glittering silver outfit, with perfectly styled platinum hair, rushed up to them.

"Mr. Mayor," she pleaded in a sotto-voce tone. "Perhaps we could take this offline, so to speak. Let's get Lillian into the hall and get the event back on track. If we could maybe clear the central carpet?" she pleaded, batting her eyelashes to try to deflect from the fact that she was telling the mayor what to do.

"Alright," he agreed grumpily.

To May's substantial relief, the woman that she guessed must be the function organizer drew her and the mayor aside, with a firm hand on each of their backs as she ushered them away. After waving to another person that May guessed was the lights and music technician, she hastily escorted them on a path through the tables and on a route that led to a side room. Behind May, the music started up again and this time, she heard flawless soprano tones peal out as Lillian made her official entrance.

The short walk had done nothing to calm down Mayor Tillman, May saw, as the organizer drew them into a side room. As soon as the door was closed, he turned to her and let rip.

"How dare you do this to me? What the hell do you think you're doing, Deputy? Did you intentionally set out to sabotage my fundraiser? Or is this just another example of your blinding incompetence?"

"It was unintentional," she tried to explain. "I didn't know I was going to walk in just as the singer was introduced. I was aiming to come in quietly, find the person I need, and speak with him discreetly. I didn't realize I was going to be spotlighted."

"Well, you sure were!" the mayor was shouting. He looked as though he was about to burst a blood vessel. May had never seen him so angry. "My biggest event of the year, and you go and show up here and turn it into a laughingstock!"

The organizer nodded loyally.

May decided she'd apologized enough. It was time, now, to push forward with the case.

"I'm here to interview a suspect," she explained calmly. "I want to talk to the owner of the properties bordering the affected homes. He's one of your guests tonight."

"And who would that be?"

"Ian Arnott," May said.

She could have predicted this wouldn't help matters, but she had no idea that the mayor would turn crimson with rage.

"Ian Arnott? This is a joke, right? This is absolutely unthinkable. He's one of the town's most solid supporters. He pays his rates on time, and he is a fine, upstanding citizen! In fact, he himself has spoken to me about his deep worry that one of his properties will be impacted next. He's highly concerned about all of this! He's been pressuring me to find the killer, ever since the first murder was called in. He's called me at least five times. He's asked me about this twice tonight already. The only other person who's called me more often is Patrick Callaway, his neighbor, and the two have already said they will put their differences aside and do whatever it takes to help. So now you're not looking so clever, are you?"

May felt a pang of doubt. This really was not going her way. Not at all. But she had to push on now. Just because the mayor thought Arnott was a good person didn't mean he couldn't also be the killer. He could be presenting this cooperative front to make sure people believed he was innocent.

"I'm not arresting him, Mayor Tillman. I am simply questioning him in order to progress the case."

"That's not why police turn up at an event like this. I know how you people work. You're looking to accuse him of the crimes. Don't try and convince me otherwise!"

"I just want to—" May began, but she didn't get to finish.

"You're embarking on a deliberate campaign to undermine my good work in this town and slander the names of my supporters! I can tell, without a doubt, you did all of this intentionally," Tillman ranted.

Then the mayor clenched his lips together. He turned angrily to the organizer.

"I'll tell you what," he said. "I'll tell you what. Bring Mr. Arnott in here. It will be interesting for him to see what happens when a deputy is fired for acting irresponsibly."

May felt a shiver of dread. With the mayor ranting on, it would be impossible for her to ask what she needed, even if she was face-to-face with the suspect.

The organizer turned away with a nod. Her face showed no sympathy for May. Nobody here was on her side. Nobody.

The mayor folded his arms and shot May a look of triumph.

"I hope you realize that your childish playground tactics to ruin my fundraiser have backfired," he said. "For someone like you who's so incompetent, the consequences are going to be brutal, but well-deserved."

"I'm simply doing my job," May said, but inside she felt as if she was dissolving. His criticism was unrelenting, and she had the horrible feeling that if she had made a mistake, she wasn't going to be able to come back from this.

The organizer returned, walking ahead of a tall, smug man with dark hair. He had a trim, well-groomed appearance and was dressed in a charcoal gray evening suit and carrying a cocktail. His expression as he came in was one of respectful anticipation.

"Mr. Tillman. What is this about?" he asked, sounding politely concerned.

"This deputy has arrived here wanting to pin these crimes on you. On you! She wants to question you in connection with the murders," Tillman said, pointing at May.

"Me?" Arnott said, sounding surprised. Was he surprised enough, May wondered.

"Yes, you. Can you believe this?"

Arnott shrugged. "The police are clearly desperate if they're looking to accuse the owners of the properties. Are you not making progress?" he said to May. "I've asked my friend here numerous times if this is solved yet. You can't believe the stress I'm going through, thinking that at any time he could strike in one of my rental homes."

"But there hasn't been a murder at your rentals," May pointed out. "Only at those of your rival's homes and neighboring those."

"So, you say that means I'm a killer?" Arnott wrinkled up his nose in disbelief as he stared at May. "You'll have to do better than that if you're going to find this murderer. Are these police for real?" he said to the mayor. "This woman's been on the case for how long, and she hasn't managed to find the killer?"

"She won't be on the case much longer," the mayor threatened.

"Where were you earlier this evening?" May pressured Arnott, wanting the facts.

"I was at home, preparing for this function," he shot back. "My home is in downtown Cole Hill, nowhere near the affected area." He sipped his drink, looking smug.

That wasn't an alibi and May felt a flare of hope that she was on the right track, however rocky a road it was. But then, sounding furious now Arnott continued. "I can tell you now, Deputy, I am going to bring a lawsuit against you for this inconvenience, for infringing on my human rights, for unnecessary interference, and looking to smear my good name. It's quite clear the killer is a squatter. Not everyone maintains adequate security in their establishments like I do."

Now May could see the anger simmering under his urbane front. But the idea about the squatter was interesting. She wanted to ask him more about it, but he continued, now in a blatantly threatening tone.

"I'm going to sue the pants off you and I'm only going to drop the case if your boss lets you go. This is incompetence at its finest. I have had enough of it."

"I'll support you in that litigation," the mayor promised. "We should have leaned on that sheriff to bring the FBI in immediately instead of allowing this clown to mess around."

"Agreed. I'm calling my lawyer right now. He can get busy with the case so long," Arnott said.

"Did you not do your research before you came here?" the mayor asked.

May looked around at the three accusatory faces—including the event organizer—all staring at her.

"I have come here to question you, and I need to question you, Mr. Arnott," she said firmly, even though it took all her courage to stand up to the men. "If you don't want to speak to me here, or I find you're being uncooperative, we will need to go to the police department. Tonight."

"I am not the killer, as you will find out. And you'll be speaking to my lawyer next," he said, seemingly not at all worried.

This had turned into the biggest possible disaster. Her job, and the police department's reputation, were on the line now, and all thanks to her own efforts in solving the case. It wasn't fair at all but May knew she had now angered very influential people who had taken sides and joined ranks against her.

If Arnott was the killer, she was going to have to fight a battle to prove it. If he wasn't the killer, she was in a shed-load of trouble and would be sued—no matter how unfair, it would still have consequences and incur expenses for the department. Lawsuits were often unpredictable.

And then, just as May was realizing there was no easy way out of the situation she'd gotten herself into, her phone started to ring loudly.

It was Kerry on the line.

May felt like a drowning woman clutching at a life raft. Was it possible Kerry had found something that might just allow her to deflect this potential bombshell?

Of course, if Kerry was calling to say she'd found nothing, that would be worst-case a hundred times over. But right now, it was her only possible chance.

"If you don't mind," she said quickly to the mayor, "I just have to take this call."

CHAPTER TWENTY THREE

May picked up Kerry's call, saying a quick prayer that it would save her from this chaos. She was just an innocent deputy doing her job, but boy had she ended up making the wrong people mad.

May knew only too well what political pressure and the threat of litigation would do. She might not actually lose her job. They were a small police department and because they worked closely with their community, litigation was very rare and always frowned upon.

All these thoughts raced through her mind as she answered, conscious of three impatient people waiting while she spoke.

"Kerry?" she said, her voice quivering.

"May." She guessed Kerry picked up on how she sounded because her next words were, "Can you talk?"

"I can listen. I'm…er…in a meeting," May said.

"Right. Gotcha." She knew Kerry had instantly picked up on the situation. "Well, I got together with one of our IT guys who's very good at research, and together we brainstormed and went into our databases."

"Did you find anything?" May asked.

"Yeah, we did. And it's pretty interesting."

"What've you found?" May asked.

"Your suspect doesn't have any arrests in Minnesota. But he has—shall we say—made unwise choices while vacationing."

"In what way?" May asked.

"He was arrested in the raid of a Hawaii brothel last year," Kerry said. "He claimed he'd walked into it accidentally while on a business trip. The same thing happened when he was in Texas recently. And a woman in a hotel in Orlando, Florida, laid charges of harassment because he was drunk and soliciting her. They settled out of court. So, that's the criminal side. Additionally, there are some online activities that my colleague has also picked up on. Membership of various sites the FBI is watching. He generally goes under the avatar name of "Spanky Sam," if you're interested."

"Spanky Sam?" May said aloud, feeling shocked.

The effect those words had on Ian Arnott was instant.

He dropped his cocktail glass, which shattered on the floor with a crash. He took a step back, looking suddenly pale and haunted.

"Oh, Mr. Arnott, I'm so sorry. I'll get that cleaned up straight away," the organizer said, rallying round as if it had been her fault and not his. She rushed out of the room.

"I'll send all the info to you now, in an email," Kerry said. "Just in case you need it."

"That's great, thank you," May said, remembering to sound professional and as if she wasn't wrapping up a call with her sister, but rather with an anonymous, high-up, FBI connection.

She cut the call and turned back to the two men.

Mayor Tillman looked ready to continue the fight, but Arnott, on the other hand, looked totally crestfallen. He'd clearly joined the dots and realized that May had been doing out-of-state research on him and that she'd most likely picked up everything there was to find.

She could see in his face that this was all so potentially embarrassing, not to mention damaging to his status and reputation in the town since there had been actual arrests made. And clearly, he didn't want it to go any further.

"You know," he said hastily, "I've rethought."

"You've what?" Tillman turned to him looking appalled, as if he'd just been deserted by his troops on the frontline.

Looking directly at May, and now with a pleading expression in his eyes, Arnott continued. "I think I lost my temper there for a moment. I've been under a lot of stress with these murders. But now that I'm calmer, I realize this brave lady is doing a fine job."

"She's what?" Tillman said incredulously.

"I'll be happy to accompany you for questioning immediately, ma'am," Arnott said, giving her a respectful nod that was a world away from the contemptuous glare he'd shown her a minute ago. "This is a serious matter. It's only right that you do whatever it takes." Arnott spoke in deferential tones that were totally at odds with the manner he'd shown May just a few minutes ago.

May nodded politely. "I'm glad you're ready to talk. Let's take a walk to the car. It'll be quieter in the police department," she said, wanting to get him and herself away from the mayor while the going was good. She turned to the organizer, who'd bustled back in with one of the waiters, carrying a dustpan and brush. "Perhaps you'd like to walk out with us?" she asked the glittery dressed woman.

May didn't want to be alone with this suspect, in a situation where he might be able to make a run for it. As of yet, there was not sufficient proof to handcuff him, and in any case, May didn't want to do that here.

But, as she and Arnott wove their way through the tables, May sent a quick text to the officer at the Cole Hill police department.

"Backup vehicle needed urgently at Three Trees Lodge. Please send an officer out asap. Emergency."

She did not trust Arnott not to try and flee. She wasn't going to let him out of her sight. Most likely, he'd do nothing in public, given his importance and social standing in the community. But if it was only the two of them, she knew all bets would be off.

So now, like a game of chess, May needed to make sure that the pieces were where they needed to be so that she could make sure she didn't lose her suspect.

When they reached the lobby, she asked the organizer, "Would you mind stepping outside for a moment?"

"Sure, sure. I'll do that," the woman said.

That gave her and Arnott privacy, in the lobby, with the organizer outside, unknowingly guarding the exit point. It would buy her some time until the backup car arrived to help take him in.

And in any case, she now realized, Mr. Arnott was very eager to speak to her. Extremely keen, in fact.

As soon as they were alone in the lobby, he stammered, "Look, I know you must have checked up on me. I…er…I had marital problems a while back. I did some things I definitely regret. I've mended my ways, of course."

"Of course," May said, in a tone of polite disbelief.

"I didn't do these murders. I don't have anyone who can account for my movements earlier today, though."

"And last night?"

Arnott squirmed, shifting from foot to foot.

"I live alone since the divorce earlier this year," he admitted. "My movements in the evening…er…can't really be accounted for. I'll…I'll do my best. There may be some emails I've answered, that can provide proof."

Or else his nighttime activities last night involved more of the same that Kerry had uncovered, May thought.

He was still a suspect. She still wanted to question him very closely and was by no means letting him off the hook. But now, looking at his genuine embarrassment, she thought that his attack on her earlier might have been prompted by the guilt over his other activities.

She was beginning to think that although not innocent, he might not be the one she was looking for. His misdemeanors were of the wrong type. She was not going to rule him out, though, but was going to keep the pressure on him as much as she could, until he either confessed, or she found a suspect that fit the picture more accurately.

At that moment, lights blazed, and the backup car flew up the driveway, stopping outside the venue, lights flashing. Two officers climbed out.

"Please could you take this gentleman to the department for questioning," May called to them, making sure to be polite since the organizer was listening. Then she turned to Arnott.

"Please go with the officers," May said politely. "Everything that we discuss in questioning will remain entirely confidential if it is not directly relevant to the case. Thank you for your cooperation."

"Understood," he said doubtfully.

"I'll join you at Cole Hill in a few minutes, and you are most welcome to contact your lawyer in the meantime," May said.

Did she see a flash of gratitude in his eyes? At any rate, weirdly, Ian Arnott was almost behaving as if he owed her one. What a turnaround.

"I'll see you there just now, but there's a place I need to go first," May added.

She watched as Arnott walked obediently between the two officers and climbed into the car. It drove off, lights now no longer flashing.

May climbed into her own car.

Before she went to the police department and it got too late, she wanted to explore the suggestion that Arnott had made earlier about the squatter. Perhaps he'd just been saying it to try and point blame at his rival, but what if that suggestion was based on something he'd noticed, seen, or heard about?

She could ask him more during the questioning, but then another idea occurred to her. Since she was passing close to the homes, perhaps she could go and see for herself if what he'd said was true.

Now that the seed of the idea had been planted in her mind, May was wondering if the historic homes had another illegal tenant, one who currently lived in one of these old homes.

Perhaps he was the one who had been seen and heard and was now killing to protect his own environment. And if there was such a person, she was sure she knew which home he'd be hiding in.

With that idea in mind, May climbed into her car and sped off, heading for the historic district.

CHAPTER TWENTY FOUR

Kate cowered against the basement's back wall, listening to the footsteps return, the only light being the faint beam shone by her phone. This man, this killer, was going to try again, she knew it. He had been quiet for a long time, an hour or two perhaps, but she'd been too scared to move her barricades because he'd told her he was still there, waiting.

She'd shouted and screamed for help until she was hoarse, but the room was too remote, too far under the ground, and no help had arrived.

Her fiancé was out of town, or he would have been wondering where she was by now. But her work colleagues would only look for her tomorrow.

Tomorrow would be too late. Right now, this monster wanted to break into the room and murder her.

There was a crash against the door, and she let out another shriek. He was doing exactly what she'd feared. He was going to break in, and he was going to get to her. The door was old, built when they'd built this house, and it certainly wasn't going to withstand an assault much longer.

"Don't let him get to me," she pleaded to the darkness, whispering "no" to herself over and over again.

She was almost sobbing with fear. She was going to die. He was going to kill her.

A second crash against the door sent splinters of wood flying into the room.

"Leave! Leave!" Kate cried.

She was on her own. She had to get herself out of this, somehow. She thought of her sister, her fiancé. What would they say if they knew what she was going through now?

Would she live to see the morning light? Or was her time about to run out?

Her loved ones would tell her to do whatever she could to protect herself, she decided. And that meant barricade the door, Kate decided. It opened inwards. If she could block it, then he wouldn't be able to get past.

And there was plenty of furniture here. She just had to use it. Drag it to the door. Get it in place.

Having something to do helped numb her terror. She shone her phone's flashlight around the cluttered basement as a third crash made her jump. She didn't have much time. Not much time at all.

But here was a big, solid item of furniture. An old wine rack, from the look of things. If she could push it to the door, she could wedge it in place.

A plan was forming in her mind. Desperate, probably crazy, but a plan at least. A way she might save herself.

She grabbed the dusty wine rack and began tugging and pulling at it with all her might.

It was heavy. Really heavy. Kate's legs were trembling as if she had been running for miles. But she refused to give up. She had to try to keep shoving at the wine rack, keep trying to drag it across the room. There it was, slowly moving, inching its way across the floor, wood screaming and protesting.

She pushed it in place, gasping with the effort. She propped up a plank which she then wedged against a ridge in the floor.

Then she grabbed another, smaller piece of furniture, one of those old sideboards, and pushed that into place too. The two pieces of furniture, braced by the plank, formed a barrier against the door. Kate was gasping for breath, exhausted. But at least she now knew that the door was reasonably safe, for a while at least.

She tried again to use her phone but there was still no signal.

Kate listened hard. The crashing against the door had stopped. Had he gone away? She hadn't heard him leave. But perhaps he had walked away.

The thought of him lying in wait for her was too horrifying to contemplate. There was no way she could open the door now. No way. She was holed up in here, for days if needed, until the police got here, until someone came looking for her.

But Kate was prepared to wait. To save her life, she could be patient. As patient as it took. She might be a little thirsty, but she could survive for a couple of days. Perhaps phone signal would improve in the morning.

And she could yell as soon as she heard the sound of anyone on the floor above her.

But then, Kate realized she was hearing another sound. A strange, scraping, scratching noise. Metal on metal. It was coming from the far wall of the basement, near the ceiling.

Fear flooded her again. What was it? What was going on?

Barely daring to breathe, she tiptoed over to have a look and see if she could figure it out.

Shining the phone flashlight up, she saw that small rivers of dust were being dislodged from a large metal compartment in the wall.

Abruptly she realized what it was. This was a large ventilation grille, set in the wall. In the dark, she hadn't even noticed it was there. He'd gone outside and found where it led. And now he was working at it. Loosening it. It was more than big enough for a man to climb through, she realized with a rush of horror.

And, as she thought this, the grille was pushed out of place and fell into the room. Kate leaped aside with a scream, out of its path, and it landed on the floor with a heavy clang.

Kate shrieked in fear, because there he was, a foot appearing and an arm, and then his face, a pale blur in the almost dark. He was coming in!

She grabbed a piece of wood, threw it at him, but it didn't stop him. Her breath was panting in her lungs. She couldn't fight him off. Couldn't hold him back.

And she'd just blocked the only way out. She'd blocked her exit route, her only means of escaping him.

Now crying with fear, Kate rushed to the contraption she'd set up at the door. She got hold of the sideboard and tugged with all her might, trying to move it away.

"Please, move. Please, move," she begged the heavy furniture, feeling her nails chip and tear as she battled with the even heavier wine rack, which was now so close to the door she couldn't get a grip on it.

She knew she didn't have time. But somehow, she managed to move it enough to squeeze past. Kate scrabbled in the lock, trying to get the key in. She didn't dare to look behind her. All she could do was hope she'd be fast enough.

Perhaps she'd make it out in time.

And then there was a soft thump behind her. Kate's mind froze. It couldn't be. He couldn't be in the room already. Her nerves were on fire. Her skin was crawling with horror.

The key slid, turned. She had done it.

She yanked the door open and began rushing up the stairs. She'd made it, she was going to get away, she'd been able to do it in time.

But as she got halfway up the stairs, with a loud thump of footsteps, she heard him in pursuit. The murderer. He was right behind her.

She didn't think she could go faster, but her own terror lent her a new turn of speed. She raced upstairs, hearing her own thudding footsteps in the night as she made it to the front door, and ran outside.

Her car key. Where was it?

Her heart jolted as she realized it was in her purse. Back in the house. She'd left her purse in the hallway, she'd put it down when taking the first photo.

And there was no time now to call for help because he was coming after her, his bulky shape framed in the doorway, heading inexorably in her direction with a big, splintered piece of wood in his hand.

Tears streaming from her eyes, Kate fled into the night.

CHAPTER TWENTY FIVE

As she sped to the historic district, May was disturbed to realize that she wasn't as sure about Ian Arnott's guilt as she thought she had been. He was definitely a lover of sleaze, a bully, and a man who'd take a chance and pressurize with a lawsuit. He wasn't a nice person but having been face-to-face with him and seeing how he reacted to her, May acknowledged reluctantly that being a dislikeable man didn't mean he was the killer.

She still needed to question him, but before she did that, she wanted to find out more about the homes by going there and seeing for herself.

Arnott had mentioned a squatter. Dale Crain had said to her that the homes had been haunted, and that number four Windrush had been the most haunted. And the guests at the writing retreat had definitely seen and heard activity in the house. They'd told her about something else too.

And May was realizing now that she had misunderstood them.

The brunette had said, "They said the house has an old basement. I remember hearing about a secret room."

May had thought she was referring to the same place. But what if she'd understood her wrong, and she'd been saying there were two hidden places within this house? What if there was a secret room, in addition to the basement, that May had missed?

She wanted to check out the place more closely before heading to the police department. She knew Ian Arnott wouldn't mind the wait. In fact, May suspected that Ian Arnott would be very, very patient and uncomplaining while he waited, thanks to the dirt she had on him now.

But May was starting to think that she was looking for someone less normal seeming than Arnott. Someone who was not operating in a logical mindset or even a functional member of society. A man who felt drawn or bound to these houses, who had been lurking and lingering in the area for a while.

It was a strong hunch, but May knew a hunch was drawn from information that had been observed and taken in. It was not just a random suspicion. She was acting on her instincts, but they were being guided by the information she'd picked up on the case so far.

It was getting late into the night now, after nine p.m. Her hands tight on the wheel, May turned onto the road where the first two murders had taken place near the bottom of the hill.

The houses did look spooky, she thought, with their sloping roofs, their bulky shapes, their arched windows, and the feeling that they were homes of yesteryear where life and death had played out inside the walls and ghosts could linger.

There was something odd, a sense of the eerie. The houses were so large and empty. No one was around, there was no sound of life, no sign of activity. No light came from any of the windows here either.

The local police were guarding the area as best they could. May saw that a police cordon had been set up at the top of Windrush Road, and a police officer was standing by.

"Evening," she greeted the officer.

"Evening, Deputy," he replied. "Everything's quiet so far, and only a few people have been in and out. Mostly, the visitors in these few houses have been taking their possessions and leaving. I've searched all the cars carefully and noted down the number plates. No sign of any weapons that match the murder weapon's description."

"Keep up the good work and keep alert," May said. "I'm going down to do another search in number four. Do you have the key?" she asked.

"Yes, I do. He looked in his vehicle and handed her an envelope. "Here you are."

May took the key and headed down the hill. She parked on a side road closest to the writers retreat home, grabbed her flashlight, and headed for the house.

It was more than a little spooky, she thought. It was quiet, there was no traffic noise here in this cul-de-sac, just the unearthly quiet of the old houses, which must have been this way for centuries.

The wind had started up again and was gusting in the tall trees. The houses were dark and brooding, the only sign of brightness was the yellow crime scene tape.

Somewhere around here, a killer had been lurking, she thought. Somewhere around here, he was watching the house. And perhaps he had been hiding inside.

Of course, that meant that she'd risk bumping into him. But she had to check. Her hunch was strong enough to be worth doing that.

Taking a deep breath, she ducked under the crime scene tape, opened the heavy front door of number four, and walked into the home.

It was pitch dark and May shivered. The house felt strangely cold, and she had a sense of foreboding that prickled its way down her spine.

But she couldn't allow herself to be put off by a fear of ghosts. Ghosts did not kill, May told herself. Real, alive humans did, and that's who she was looking for.

Would she find him in here, or any signs of him, if she searched thoroughly enough?

May had a short debate with herself over whether or not she should turn on the lights. In the end, she decided against it. Lit up like a Christmas tree, this house would send a clear message that somebody was in here. It would be better to use her flashlight and remain under the radar, May decided. Even though there was a police cordon at the top of the road, the killer might have avoided it.

The killer might be in here, holed up and alone.

Or he might be out searching for fresh victims. New kills, she thought with a chill.

She turned on her flashlight, feeling briefly awed by the size and construction of this huge, elegant home. It was full of character and complexity, and as an older home, it also had many nooks and crannies, many passages, and many closets and rooms tucked away.

It was a home to be proud of, a home that one could easily love, and now as she stood here, trying to get into the killer's mind, May was wondering if the killer himself also loved this home, and if he felt a twisted need to protect it from people that he saw as invading it.

May had a moment of doubt, of second-guessing herself, but she pushed it aside as she paced into the home, shining her flashlight carefully around, trying to think like the killer would.

Every creak, every sound made her jump, but she refused to let her fear overcome her. She paced through the hall, looking for any hidden doors, any places that might have been boarded off in past decades and forgotten about.

She moved through the kitchen, and then into the dining area. She had a hunch that the killer might have had his hideaway here. It had a huge bay window. Was there a hidden nook? May shone her flashlight into the darkness around the window and into the shadows of the high wooden blinds that kept the light out.

Was he watching her right now, she wondered with a flare of fear.

She shook off the fear as she paced through the dining area into the conservatory, with its glass walls and arched roof, and again into the living room.

She checked the old lounge where he'd murdered Cyndi but couldn't find anything along the walls there. She checked the victim's bedroom. She shone the light high and low, she checked behind pictures, curtains, and cupboards. Nothing.

Then, feeling puzzled and a bit deflated, although still jumpy, she moved to the upstairs area and began checking the rooms there.

Her heart hammering, her breath coming a little fast, she turned the handle and pushed open the door to the master bedroom. Would it have a closet with a false wall? Would a secret dressing room have provided a place for him?

There was nothing she could see. She moved to the other bedrooms and the bathrooms, searching carefully, but beginning to feel more and more confused, because her hunch must be wrong.

She'd guessed incorrectly.

May felt filled with frustration, because her lead hadn't panned out, and now her only option was to go back to the police department and question her suspect waiting there. Although she had no doubt that he would be fully cooperative, she sensed that the answers to this terrible crime spree lay elsewhere.

Could he have hidden out in one of the other houses, she wondered.

But this had been the house that both the writers retreat guests and Dale Crain had specifically mentioned. Dale had known the area very well. He'd seen this "ghost" recently, in the past few weeks since he'd been out of jail.

But where could this invisible man possible be hiding?

May wasn't ready to give up yet. As she puzzled over this seemingly impossible scenario, thinking over every possible angle, she suddenly realized there was one last thing she could do. One last-ditch attempt she could make.

This was the historic district. And she was going to see if history itself could give her the answers she needed. It was going to have to come from a surprising source.

Never had May thought that her own mother might be the one to help her with critical, make-or-break information on a case.

But hoping that she would, May took out her phone.

CHAPTER TWENTY SIX

Standing alone in the hallway of the old house, May listened to the phone ring, feeling uneasy. She moved so that she had her back to the wall—a wall she knew had to be solid and contained no false doors. This home felt desolate and threatening. She had the strange feeling that it was clinging tightly to its secrets, unwilling to let them go.

It made her all the more determined to prize the truth out of its hiding place, so that this beautiful area could be drawn into the present day and become the safe, scenic tourist haven that she knew it could be.

Her mother answered, and May heard a brief sound of the television in the background before it was muted.

"May! What a surprise," her mother said. "Your father and I were just finishing a movie. Is everything alright, honey?"

"Everything's fine," May said, hearing the note of anxiety in her mother's voice.

"Have you caught that killer yet? We've been hearing so much about it from Edna. She's been following the case, hoping that the district can be saved. As a historian, she's so keen to get these historic tours up and running."

"We haven't caught the killer yet," May said. "But we are getting closer, I think. That's why I'm calling you now."

Of course, her mother didn't listen, but went off on her own tangent.

"You know, I'm surprised the FBI hasn't been called in already. Don't you think you might need them at this point, sweetheart?" Mrs. Moore said in helpful tones, causing May's blood pressure to spike briefly.

But she wasn't allowing herself to be sidetracked. She needed to focus!

"I was hoping that Edna might be able to help me," May said quickly, before her mother could elaborate on the need for the FBI to help solve this crime, and how Kerry could probably catch the killer in a flash. She had a feeling that her mother had a lot more to say on this issue and she didn't want her to get started. It was highly likely that if she gained any more momentum, May wouldn't be able to stop her at all.

"Edna can help you with what, honey?" her mother asked, now sounding intrigued.

"You mentioned to me that she's a specialist on the area's history?"

"Yes, that's right, honey."

"Could you possibly give me her phone number?"

There was a pause. May guessed that her mother was boiling over with curiosity about why May needed this information. Her mother was wanting to sleuth vicariously through May, she now realized. But there wasn't time! Not when every minute counted in tracking down this man.

"Please, mom, I do need it urgently," May said. "I'll tell you exactly why later. I promise."

With a reluctant sigh, her mother abandoned the quest for more information.

"If this is all solved by tomorrow, then you must come for dinner, angel. I'll get Edna's number for you now," she agreed.

She read out the number to May.

"Thanks so much," May said. "I'll give you all the details, I promise. Tomorrow, over dinner, hopefully."

"Thanks, honey," her mother said.

May cut the call and immediately dialed Edna's number, feeling impatient and worried that this was all too late, that Edna wouldn't answer her phone, and that her last attempt at finding what she needed would fail.

It rang and rang. May was starting to hyperventilate with the stress.

Just as she thought it would go through to voicemail, it was picked up. Edna sounded bright and friendly, despite the late hour.

"Good evening," she said.

May had never met her, but from her voice, she imagined her as a sprightly, gray-haired woman with sparkling eyes and an energy and interest in the world. That was most definitely her picture of the woman she hoped would be able to help her.

Local knowledge—the most detailed, specialized local knowledge possible—was the key to this case. May was sure of it.

"Good evening, Edna. It's Deputy May Moore here. I'm sorry to be calling so late."

"Oh, May Moore!" Edna sounded enthusiastic at the sound of May's name. "You're Mrs. M's daughter and with the local police, aren't you? How can I help?"

"It's about the murders taking place in the historic district," May said.

"Yes, such a terrible thing. That's my area of specialization, that architecture," Edna said. "I was consulted by a couple of the new owners wanting to renovate, to ensure they maintained the historic character and integrity of the homes."

"Do you have any of the old plans for number four?" May said, crossing her fingers. "Because I am hoping that we can help track down the killer by locating his hiding place."

"Number four?" Edna said, sounding thoughtful. "Now that really is an interesting home."

"Why is that?"

"There's a basement that's very difficult to access. In fact, it's only accessible now through the kitchen fireplace, which is not often used. I'm sure if you're looking for a hiding place, that would be it," she said.

"Yes, I have already found the basement. Unfortunately, there's no sign that the killer was ever down there. The dust looked undisturbed," May said.

"What a pity. But let me look back. There was some other interesting feature, I do recall that. Let me see what it was. Hold on a minute."

May waited, feeling impatient but hopeful as Edna checked back through her records. She heard the flipping of pages and imagined Edna looking through an old, dusty volume of plans or drawings.

"Ah, here it is!" she said. "It's a fascinating fact actually. There was a secret wine cellar that was built literally inside of the house in 1920, which we guess must have been during the Prohibition era. It's likely that it was used to keep a secret stash of wine and spirits and most likely to hold gatherings where alcohol was consumed. It was a small, well-hidden speakeasy."

"So, it was big enough to contain a few people?" May asked, needing to get a picture of whether the killer could have used it as a base.

"Yes, the size of a small room, I believe. The records here say, 'it had a wall filled with bottle racks, a long table and a bench that could seat eight.' There was even a tiny washroom so that guests could stay hidden for many hours without needing to go back into the main house. So, I guess, a few square yards?"

May's eyebrows rose. She felt sure that if she could access this secret room, it would lead her to the killer. Now, she strongly suspected he had discovered this cellar and was using it.

"How was it accessed?" she asked.

"Well, that's the difficult part. It doesn't say here. It just says it was in the downstairs area of the house, obviously. Not the kitchen, from what I can see here, because the basement is under the kitchen. From what I can deduce, that means it must have been in the old lounge."

That was exactly where Cyndi had been murdered! This was all adding up, May realized.

"And it doesn't say where the door is?" May asked.

"I believe it's only accessible if you know it's there, which you don't unless you're told and know exactly where to look," she said, sounding pleased with herself. "That's what this old book says, at any rate."

"Have you still got a copy of the plans, Edna?" she asked.

"Of course, I do. I'm a historian," Edna said, sounding proud. "The whole reason I have compiled the plans is to make sure the renovations are done to the highest possible standards in a historically accurate way. This can't be done unless the whole house is treated as a historic site. I keep them locked up safely, of course. I'm not that much of a daredevil to leave them lying around."

May's heart began to beat faster. It seemed she was on the right track, after all.

"Could you send them to me?" May asked, wondering if seeing the plans would help her gain access.

"I can, but the problem is that the cellar is not listed on the original plans. I only added it into my record of the home as a result of my extensive reading."

May's heart thumped all the way down again.

"So, you don't think the door will be visible from anywhere?" she asked, disappointed.

"Unfortunately, there's no record of it. It might have been bricked up years ago. Of course, being a speakeasy, it would have been very well-concealed to start with."

A secret room under the place where the killer had struck. No sign of any doorways.

But May suddenly had an idea. Logically, if she'd been the owner of this home and the builder of the cellar, she knew how she would have done it.

"I think you've been a great help," she told Edna. "I'm going to check something out, based on what you've said."

"I hope you find it, and do let me know," Edna agreed.

May cut the call and put her phone away.

This time, she knew exactly where she was going to focus her hunt.

She'd been looking in all the wrong places and had missed the most obvious one at all. Now, it was time to see if her theory was correct.

CHAPTER TWENTY SEVEN

May rushed back to the lounge, her feet thudding on the floorboards, feeling as if this was truly her last-ditch attempt. This was her only remaining chance to find out who this killer was. She knew without a doubt that he would kill again. If he couldn't find anyone in his immediate neighborhood, he would look further afield. May didn't doubt it.

Serial killers always did that. Once the lust for blood had overtaken them it seemed that the reasons for their killing became less important, and the kill itself began to be the main goal in their twisted minds.

But now, May was on the hunt for his hiding place.

The old cellar, built as a speakeasy during Prohibition, was surely where he'd made his lair. She'd been looking for doors in walls and had overlooked the most obvious location, the one that the owner surely would have thought of when he constructed his underground room.

A door in the floor.

That was what she was looking for now, as she re-entered the cluttered lounge, hearing the faint creaking of the thick, old floorboards.

Now, May knew she had to go with the idea that the floorboards themselves were the hiding place.

She felt sure that she must be on the right track, and that the secret door was here somewhere. She was looking for a trapdoor, perhaps concealed under a rug, or disguised as a part of the floorboards. It might even be so well-hidden as to be invisible, and she was sure it wouldn't be simple to open.

Perhaps she was looking for a single floorboard, perhaps one with slightly different coloring, that might activate a hidden hatch.

She crouched down, and began to search, feeling with her hands along each of the floorboards, listening out carefully for any sounds from below, because she had no doubt that if she found what she was looking for, she would be accessing the killer's secret hideaway, and there was a chance he could be inside.

"Where are you hiding? I'm going to find you and I'm not going to give up," she muttered to herself as she searched.

May scoured the lounge with her hands, feeling every inch of the floor, not wanting to miss the tiniest detail or the smallest knot in the wood. She felt determined to find her prize.

She searched and searched, feeling her way methodically along the floor, with her heart speeding up every time she felt an unevenness in the floor, and then disappointment flooding back again as she failed to activate any openings.

She was beginning to think she was going to get nowhere, and that her idea had been completely wrong, when she felt an indentation in the floorboard close to the old floral sofa.

May felt around the floorboard, pressing and pushing.

Then, she heard a soft click, and the floorboard moved slightly. She felt something under it, something small and metallic. Was it a lever of some kind?

At first, May thought she had imagined it, but when she pressed down on the hidden lever, she heard a creaking, grinding sound.

She gasped, as a section of the floor opened and moved smoothly downward, as if a hidden lever must have activated a larger hatch.

She stared down, into the blackness of the cellar.

Had she really uncovered the killer's hiding place? She couldn't believe she had actually done it and was now looking at a dark opening that had remained secret and invisible for many years—except to the killer.

An old steel ladder was attached to the side of the wall.

Before she climbed down, May shone her flashlight, feeling nervous at the thought that he might be waiting. But she couldn't hear so much as a breath coming from down below.

She could make out the building's sounds, the creaking of floorboards upstairs in the house, and the sound of the night wind outside. But the space down the ladder seemed completely silent.

He might come back at any moment, though, so the sooner she took a look around, the better. Hopefully, something in here would point the way to his identity, or better yet, his whereabouts.

Bracing herself, May stepped down the ladder and into the cellar, which was lit by a single bulb. With a shaking hand, she turned on the dim light and stared around.

It smelled damp, and she thought there was still a faint fragrance of old wine imbued in the wooden panels of the walls. The table and the wine racks that Edna had spoken about were no longer there. Instead, there was a steel chest, a small desk, and a single bed. There were earplugs and earmuffs on the pillow. Clearly, this man—this psychopath—had very sensitive hearing. May guessed that would be an asset to him in his kills. If his ears were keen, he'd be able to pick up the noises of his prey easily.

May's eyes widened as she saw a notebook on the table. Quickly pulling on a glove to protect this important piece of evidence, she opened it, wondering if it might contain anything useful.

It was filled with strange scrawlings, weird drawings, and nonsensical patterns that she couldn't figure out. May paged through, looking at the few excerpts that made sense. It felt fascinating, yet repelling, to have this clear of a window into this man's damaged mind.

I spoke to Old Man tonight. His voice sounded like the wind in the trees and he spoke of sorrow.

I communicated with Little Woman this afternoon, and her tones were as clear as a bell.

It sounded as if he was communicating with imaginary people. Ghosts, perhaps. That was why he was drawn to this district, May reasoned. But then, the tone of the scrawling changed and there were angry phrases.

The noises! They are disturbing these spirits, and I can't hear them! Number 5, I must go to Number 5!

May's eyebrows rose. That was the first murder site. He'd written it down. Did he mention the others? Did he mention where he was now?"

With shaking hands, she turned the pages, hoping for some clue, some indication of where he might be.

She saw that the murder he'd committed here was not mentioned. Perhaps it had been a spur of the moment crime. But the other house was mentioned.

Bangs, thumps, music! I know where it's coming from! It's coming from Number 6, across the river. I will find the cause, so they can be at peace again!

May narrowed her eyes. Number six hadn't been affected. It hadn't been the scene of a kill. As far as she recalled, that home had been empty when she'd arrived. It was the home next door, Number seven, where the elderly lady had been killed.

So, maybe the killer had found nobody in the target property and had done what she expected him to start doing. He'd expanded his hunt and looked for anyone nearby to kill.

Turning the page again, she peered down at the crooked, scrawled words.

Aurora! I will clean you now. The sounds will disappear. I am strong! I am strong and I will cleanse you!

May shivered. It was all jumbled, like somebody who talked to themselves.

Noise louder than ever! But the spirits can no longer be heard!

Now May understood why he had been so angry. And here was the last page, the final page with writing.

I'm getting mad, and I'm worried I will never hear the voices again. They must show me the way.

May peered at the almost illegible words, knowing she needed to make sense of them.

There is someone in Number 14. All the way down the road! And they are the one. The one who has been doing all of this. They are the one who must be stopped.

May's eyes widened, as she realized that this man had surely given her the location of his next victim.

Number fourteen, which was a couple of blocks away and on the other side of the small lake, was the destination he was now staking out. It was farther than he'd been before. He was expanding his territory.

He could already be there! May clambered back up the ladder, the secret trapdoor slamming shut behind her.

She ran at full speed out through the house, almost tripping on the rug, as she bolted for the door. It might already be too late to stop this desperately deluded man from murdering again, but if she possibly could, May was going to try.

CHAPTER TWENTY EIGHT

As she raced for the narrow road leading across the lake, May got on her cellphone. Her first call was to Owen.

"May! I'm stuck in the press conference, but if there's an emergency, I'll run out," he muttered in a soft voice.

"I've found him!" she said breathlessly. "It's an emergency! He's targeting house number fourteen next. That's where he's going to be. I'm on my way there now. Please, get there as fast as you can, and call for more backup! There are police at the top of the road, but this is on a different road, across the lake."

"I'm on my way!" Speaking louder now, she could hear Owen was causing a commotion. "Sorry, I have to leave! Sorry, there's a police emergency. I've been called out. Police emergency! 'Scuse me please!"

She could hear a chorus of raised voices, anxious words, a hubbub in the background, and then the call cut out.

May threw the phone back into her pocket, and turned all her energy back to running, heading down the hill, desperate to reach the house.

Her feet were slipping and skidding on the gravel path that led down to the scenic road crossing, and she felt scared and very much alone, knowing that she'd be the only person arriving at this scene. But she had to get there before the killer did his deadly work once more.

There was number fourteen, ahead. Who was here? Someone was here. Several people, in fact. There were cars parked all around the driveway.

May rushed up the path to the front door. What was playing out in here? Was the killer hiding away somewhere and waiting to strike? She could hear voices and music coming from inside.

Reaching the door, May hammered on it, breathing hard.

After a pause, a man opened the door. He looked about twenty, casually dressed in jeans and a t-shirt, and he peered at her carefully before opening the door fully.

"Hello," he said when he saw her. "What's up? Is there a problem?"

"Your house. I'm worried it might be targeted next by the man who's been on a crime spree in the area," May gasped.

"Our house? But we only just got back, like, five minutes ago. We've been out visiting friends. There's definitely nobody in here."

"Was there any sign of forced entry?" May asked.

"No, it was all locked up. We left the doors locked and the windows all closed, with the curtains drawn, because of all the crime that's been happening across the lake. And we checked the house when we got back. All good, I think?" he said, raising an eyebrow.

"I'm not convinced. There's a police cordon at the top of the other road. Please, call Cole Hill and ask them to deploy that officer here. He can search the house. This killer knows these properties well and might be hiding somewhere. Please, until the police get here, can you all stay in one room and be on full alert. This truly is a question of life or death," May pleaded.

The man turned a few shades paler at this statement. He nodded somberly.

"Thanks for the warning. We'll do that. We'll wait for the police and stay together until we're sure it's safe."

May didn't want to wait in the house with them because a horrible idea had just occurred to her.

She was worried that the killer had done what he'd done once before. Finding that there was no suitable victim in the house he'd targeted, he might have looked nearby.

The surrounding properties were where he would have searched, just as he'd done the last time. So, this was where May needed to look, too.

Had he seen another house with people inside? His preference so far seemed to be to murder women although May guessed that could just be a coincidence.

Hurrying out of the house, she rushed over to the neighboring fence, looking over at the house next door. She could see the windows of the bedroom and the kitchen. Was there anybody there?

She saw a flash of movement. Was that a curtain twitching? Or was it her mind playing tricks on her? The house definitely seemed dark, and she didn't see any cars outside, so it was likely nobody was home. Also, narrowing her eyes in the gloom, she saw the front door looked closed.

What about the house on the other side? Had he seen an opportunity there, since the residents of number fourteen hadn't been available?

May ran down the sidewalk, looking at the home on the far side, number twelve.

There was a car parked outside the house, a small blue Honda. It had a logo on the driver's door: Cole Hill Properties Agency: Kate Toms.

That got her instincts flaring.

It looked as if Kate might have entered this house to prepare or photograph the interior.

Being in the wrong place at the wrong time might have made Kate a target. And the front door was standing open.

May's heart sank. That was not a good sign. He'd gotten inside, he must have, because any normal person would close the door behind them, especially in these times, when everyone was aware of the danger. Surely, she couldn't be too late?

She could see a few dim lights glowing from inside.

With no idea what she would find, May grabbed her gun from the holster. There was no time to be scared, no time to second guess herself. Every second was critical and could make a difference.

She burst in through the front door.

"Police!" she yelled, deciding this was no time for caution. If the killer heard her, let him come! She was ready. "Kate! Are you in here?"

She stopped in surprise as she saw that this home was mostly empty. Only a few items of furniture stood here and there, looking dusty and forlorn. Undoubtedly, this house was up for sale, and she guessed the owner was selling in a rush, probably a decision made due to the murders. That was why this estate agent had arrived here now.

"Police!" she yelled again.

May had a terrible feeling that this home was empty and that she was too late. Would she find a body here? She rushed farther inside, storming through the house, glancing into the kitchen, seeing that the lounge led out to a porch area and a huge backyard.

Could he be out there?

She noticed that steps led down to a basement room. Was he down there? As May was about to explore this possibility, she heard a faint cry.

She looked up, eyes wide, all her instincts flaring. Where had the sound come from?

It seemed to have come from outside.

May rushed to the lounge, seeing that the back door was also standing wide open. She raced out onto the porch, looking frantically around in the dark.

And then, the cry came again, and this time she saw the shapes, illuminated by the lamps along the paved path by the lake's edge.

A slender woman, who surely must be Kate, was racing to the shoreline, crying out in fear.

And behind her, she saw a tall man, running wildly in pursuit. In his hand, he was brandishing a weapon that May recognized, in the gleam of a lamp, as the white-painted wooden balustrade.

Flinging herself off the edge of the porch, May set off in pursuit. If he caught the fleeing woman now, she would die. But if May caught up first, she could prevent this.

It all hinged, now, on this final, desperate race against time.

CHAPTER TWENTY NINE

"Stop! Police!" May yelled, even though she didn't hold out much hope that the shouted word might slow the killer down. He was gaining on Kate, every one of his giant strides was taking him closer.

But her desperate yell had an effect. A surprising effect. The man broke his stride. He stumbled slightly as he turned to look at her.

For the first time she saw his face. Ghostly pale, lean and wide-eyed, May thought, in surprise, that he almost resembled one of the spirits he imagined he was communicating with.

"Stop!" she yelled again and saw him flinch.

But then, with a snarl, he turned and broke into a run again, loping along the shoreline in pursuit of the fleeing real estate agent. He was desperate to continue pursuing his victim and kill her. May had to stop him and stop him fast.

She sped up, powering after him, but she could already see that she was too far away, and he was too close to his prey. There was no way she could get close enough to stop him in time.

What could she do, how could she delay the inevitable disaster when he reached her?

"I'm coming to get you! I have a gun!" she yelled, even though she was too far away to use it in these dark surroundings and couldn't fire at a running man in poor light, especially when there was another woman beyond him also in the line of sight. "Don't make me shoot you!" she yelled, hoping to make him believe she was genuine. "I will shoot you! If you harm her, you will die!"

Every time she yelled at him, May thought she saw him tense, as if her words were literally searing him. The grass felt damp and soft under her shoes as she chased him down the hill toward the lapping waters of the lake.

But despite her best efforts, he was gaining ground, and now he'd reached her, he was there, and with a shriek, the woman was his grasp.

"Don't harm her or I will shoot!" May screamed, knowing that this was now her only hope of saving the woman.

He reached Kate, grabbed her, and swung her around. May heard her scream out in fear. It was as if her scream sent an electric shock through the killer. He convulsed, but then grabbed her tighter.

"Don't!" he warned May, in a breathless snarl. "Don't come closer. You can't shoot me now. You'll kill her. And if you try to come closer, I'll kill her."

His face drew into a mirthless grin that, with his strange, pale face, made him look like an evil clown.

May was about fifteen feet away. She was close enough that she could see Kate struggling, trying to pull away. But he was holding onto her with a strong grasp, and as May watched in horror, she shrieked again. The killer hissed, as if the sound had burned him. Frantically, one of his hands closed over her mouth.

The other was pinning her against him and the broken balustrade was grasped tight in his palm.

Her screams turned into breathless, terrified whimpers. He was going to crush the breath out of her.

"Don't hurt her!" May yelled, holding out one hand to try to draw the man's attention to her.

He stared at her, and now she saw all the madness flaring in his eyes.

"Don't shout!" he pleaded with her in a low, snarling voice. "Stop that. You're disturbing them. You're drowning out their voices and I can't hear them. I need to hear them. They always have something to say! Always!"

May gulped, trying to think of what to do. She was the detective, and he was a crazed serial killer. She had to take charge of the situation.

She kept her gun trained on him as he backed up a few strides, dragging the woman with him, out onto the pier that led a few yards out.

"Wait! Come back!" May said, but in a soft voice. "Don't hurt her. Don't hurt Kate. She's done nothing to you."

Horror flared inside her as she imagined what he might do. If he took another step back, they'd both be in the lake. Underwater, he could easily kill her within a few seconds. May didn't like her chances of rescuing a dying woman and fighting off this psychopath if he did that.

Without a doubt, the water would be the worst-case scenario, but how could she prevent this?

"I'm not going to come near you," she said, hoping to distract him, hoping not to do anything to make him nervous.

"See, you're too late," he said, grinning at her again, his voice low and snarling.

Kate started to struggle again, and he tightened his grip, making her moan in fear.

He took another step back, and she knew he was about to do it, about to launch himself into the water.

She had to keep him talking, that was the key.

"I can hear the voices too. They don't want you to go into the lake," she suggested. "It's very cold in there, and there's a chance you could drown in the waters yourself."

He stared at her blankly, as if the mention of the voices had confused his mind.

"The voices are saying, step forward so you don't fall off the edge. Let her go, and I'll walk away," she suggested, hoping against hope that this might be the right solution.

The man considered her, his gaze skittering briefly over the dark waters of the lake.

"I don't believe you," he said. But he took a step forward, a step away from that precarious edge.

Now, she had to somehow persuade him to let the victim go. May edged forward.

"Stop there!" he told her, seeing the movement instantly.

May stopped. She wasn't going to get closer. If she tried, he'd be triggered into lethal action.

"I need to take her," he mumbled to May. "I have to take her. You're causing trouble and trying to interfere. You walk away now. This one, I have to silence. She was screaming earlier. I have to silence her now."

In that moment, May realized what might work. It was the only solution she could think of. Up until now, she'd been trying to keep things quiet, trying to talk him down from his peak of murderous rage. But they'd reached a stalemate. Just now, he would be the one taking the initiative and it would not be good news.

But perhaps there was something else she could do.

And that was to make him come to her. Make herself the target. And she saw now how it could be done.

May opened her mouth and let out the biggest scream she could manage.

"I'm the noisy one!" she yelled at him. "You can never kill me! I'm going to haunt you! I'm going to be there every time you murder someone! You'll always know I'm there!"

She let out another bloodcurdling scream, and then a third, trying to psych him out, trying to provoke him into the action she needed him to take.

"You're making too much noise!" he yelled back.

"I'm using my gun!" she told him, and she had an instant of relief when she saw him flinch at that.

"I don't believe you!" he shouted back at her, his voice high and terrified.

"You're not listening to me!" she taunted him, hearing the thumping and crashing of the woman's feet as she struggled to break free of his grip.

"Shut up! Shut up! Shut up! I need to hear them! I need to hear them!"

"No! I won't!" May yelled. And then, sensing he was at tipping point, she unlocked her gun's safety and fired it once, aiming carefully for the lake's waters where the bullet could do no harm.

The sound split the air.

And finally, it cracked open the killer's control.

He did what she'd hoped he would do. He lunged toward her with a roar of rage.

He flung the woman down and she sprawled onto the jetty, sliding off the edge and, with a shriek, tipping into the deep water.

At least she was out of harm's way, May thought. For a terrible moment, she thought that the killer might go in after Kate before she had time to stop him.

But he didn't leap into the lake after her, and instead, he attacked faster than she'd believed possible.

With a bloodcurdling scream, and a whirling of limbs, he launched himself directly at May.

CHAPTER THIRTY

May knew immediately that she was fighting for her life. This man, violent and deluded, wanted only to attack. He saw her as the enemy, and he was now hell bent on committing the kill he craved.

"You're the one," he snarled at her, his teeth drawn back from his cadaver-pale face, exposing a mouth like a dark gap. "You're the one who's doing all the shouting, all the time! You're the one who's drowning out the voices!"

May tried to get her gun hand around, to aim it at him, but he was too fast. The splintered balustrade came flying down at her and she leaped aside, only the reactions of pure fear saving her from its hammering blow.

Her foot slipped and her knee slammed onto the boards, unbalancing her as she tried once again to take the shot, but he attacked too fast. Hissing in rage, he was on her. He wrenched her hand aside and his fingers bit into her wrist with numbing force. The gun dropped to the ground, clattering away on the wooden boards, lost in the darkness.

And then it was just him and her, and May could do nothing but try to fight for her life against an attacker who had tipped all the way into madness.

His hands clawed at her face, his fingernails sharp and ragged, and she twisted aside, desperate to protect herself, so that his fingers caught in her jacket instead and he wrenched at it, flinging her down to the boards as if she was nothing more than a piece of driftwood.

May rolled to save herself and as she did, tried to aim a kick at him. She was hoping to get his leg or his knee and slow him down. But she didn't manage to do more than bump his leg. With reflexes that were startlingly fast, he dodged her attack and grabbed her ankle, yanking her foot from under her and rolling her flat onto her back.

She tried to grab for his legs, but it was a moment too late. His foot was already in motion. With a vicious downward stamp, he kicked out at her. May jackknifed away and he caught her with a glancing blow on her shoulder.

She gasped in pain, and then he was on her, his hands on her throat, his knee on her chest, and May knew she had to get away from him or she'd be dead.

She tried to get her hands up, to claw at his face and his eyes, but he was too strong. With one hand still at her neck, he slapped away her hands with the other and although she was able to twist and roll her body, the power of his grip was immense.

She felt herself starting to black out, her vision blurring, and her lungs screaming for air. She grappled desperately for his wrists, trying to break his hold, trying to do anything she could to stay alive. From nearby the jetty, she heard a splashing sound and knew that the woman he'd captured was swimming for shore. She was going to be able to save herself, and if she had her head together, she might even be able to call for help.

The problem was that it would be too late for May. By the time the woman even reached the shoreline, the killer would already have done his work. Unless she could stop him. Somehow, she had to try and break out of this death grip.

"No, no, no," he kept muttering, as if he was in some kind of trance, immersed in a world of voices and sounds that no one else could hear.

May felt panic rise up inside her. She tried to shake him off, but it was no use. He was straddling her, trapping her, pinning her down, and he was suffocating her.

"No," he muttered again. And then, as if he'd heard a command, he leaned right down and stared directly into her eyes.

"You're the one I needed, the one who's going to stop this at last." He sounded triumphant.

The pressure on her throat intensified, and May kicked out again, using her fingers to tear at his hair, trying to stab him in his eyes, trying desperately to dislodge him in any way she could, but he was seemingly immune to the pain, and she still couldn't get any air into her lungs.

She kicked out, trying to throw him off balance, but it was of no use. The man was still on her and there was no escape.

And then, with that same eerie calmness, he spoke once more. "This is the end for you."

May's vision swam and for a second, she saw dark water, deep and black, opening up beneath her. She was vividly aware that she was about to pass out and that if she did, he would have won. There were only a few moments left, now. A few moments to go before he succeeded in his murderous aims.

And then, the sound of sirens shrilled from the road beyond. The police had arrived!

The only problem was that they were going to go to the house where she had directed them. They were not going to come straight down to the lake. She hadn't had the chance to redirect them.

But the sound of the sirens made the killer pause. He flinched at the noise.

"The voices! It's going to hurt them," he muttered.

For a moment, his grip on her neck loosened, and May was able to gasp in a breath of air, filtering through her bruised throat, filling her lungs. She'd had one last, life-giving sip of air, and as he gave an angry growl and tightened his grip again, May knew it was all she was going to get. But it had been enough. Enough to give her the last surge of strength and clarity she needed to try again.

May knew she had to try and save herself. She wasn't going to let this man get away to continue his killing spree. Others would die. She wouldn't be the last. He would cause untold suffering and grief.

And never mind that—what would Owen think, staring down at her body? How would her parents feel and Kerry?

Surprisingly, it was the thought of her loved ones that gave May an unexpected final surge of strength to fight.

She couldn't use her hands against him because she didn't have the power she needed to fight him. But perhaps there was something else she could use.

Reaching out, May scrabbled her fingers over the boards, feeling for her gun. Perhaps it would be in arm's reach. Her hand stretched out, hoping to find something, anything she could use.

She didn't find her gun, but she found something else, something she hadn't expected. Her fingers closed over the smooth handle of the wooden balustrade that this killer himself had used as his weapon.

She could use it too, and if she managed to time it right, she might just be able to stun him enough to get free.

Her fingers curled around the wood. She lifted it.

The killer was oblivious to what was happening. He still had his eyes locked on hers and was holding her exactly where he wanted her.

She had one chance to make her attack count. And she had to do it now.

May swung the balustrade as hard as she could. With all the power that was left in her body, she brought it down, the wooden railing cracking into his skull.

He roared in pain, his grip on her throat loosening.

May had no time to think. She scrambled away, her hands scrabbling on the wooden boards. Then, as he rose up and spun around, she pushed herself to her feet. She raised the balustrade again.

Her side was hurting, her throat was bruised, and she was light-headed from the lack of air, but she had to do what she needed. While he was still off balance, she brought the weapon down again and heard a satisfying crack as it connected with his skull.

Now, he was seriously stunned. He sprawled on the pier, breathing shallowly, his limbs moving weakly and in an uncoordinated way. And finally, she had the chance to dive down and pick up her gun.

Already, the killer was trying to scramble to his feet, but May was ready for him now.

Her voice was so hoarse she could hardly get the words out, but she managed to say, in a weak, choking voice.

"You are under arrest. Put your hands in the air. If you try to run, I will shoot."

He stared at her for a long moment, and she saw pure evil in his eyes.

"The voices will never leave me," he whispered. Then he raised his hands slowly.

And, from the road, May heard a woman's panicked voice.

"Police, police! Come quick! This way! The woman who saved me—she's being attacked! Please, come down here, quick!"

With a surge of relief, May knew that she had managed to do what it took. Kate had swum to safety and was bringing the police to the scene. Help was on the way. Owen, and backup, would be down here at the lake within a minute. And soon, this killer, who had wreaked such torment and death in this beautiful area, would be handcuffed, and on the way to prison.

The case was closed. No longer would the historic district be terrorized.

And best of all, May realized in surprise, she'd kept her promise to the mayor, and caught the murderer before the night was over.

CHAPTER THIRTY ONE

When May arrived at the police department the following morning, the first thing—or rather, the first car—she saw was the one she'd hoped never to see again.

The mayor's shiny black vehicle was parked outside the police department, and she felt a thrill of horror at the sight. He'd promised to make life hell for them, to pick their department apart, to bring May's career to a grinding halt.

Yes, they'd caught the killer, but that didn't mean the mayor's vendetta against them would stop. If they had made a lasting enemy out of him, then she knew it would mean trouble going forward for the foreseeable future.

She was later into work than usual because she'd gone past the drugstore to get medication for her sore throat. It had been recommended by the paramedics who'd checked her over late last night after they had examined Kate and found her to be healthy and unharmed.

May hoped that her tardy arrival wouldn't count against her.

Rushing into the police department, she headed straight for the back office.

There, she saw that Sheriff Jack was busy presenting a summary of the case to the mayor and two of his entourage, who were seated at the table. Owen was standing at the back of the room, together with two other officers from the Fairshore department. He gave her a worried glance.

May knew she needed to speak to Owen. There were things she needed to say to him, things that she hadn't had the time to get straight in her own head yet. She needed to fully update him on the situation with Lauren, and how she and Kerry were working together, and tell him all about the video.

With everything happening so fast, things had snowballed, and now she knew he probably feared she was hiding more.

There was still no time for that now, and she didn't know where to start. She had to find out more herself, before she was ready to share the full, complex update with Owen.

In any case there were now more serious issues waiting right in front of her.

Sheriff Jack raised his eyebrows briefly in greeting as May tiptoed in.

"So, Mayor Tillman, the suspect who was arrested last night proved to be a thirty-five-year-old drifter by the name of Ray Evans, who was originally from a neighboring town, and has been in and out of various institutions, suffering from mental illness and schizophrenia. He walked out of his treatment facility a few years ago and fell off their radar. For a while, in his twenties, he held down a job at the records archive in town and it's there that he developed an obsession with the area's history, believing that he was the only one who could speak with the dead, whose voices he could hear."

"Astounding," the mayor muttered.

"We understand, from interviewing him, that he set up a base in the underground cellar and lived there for quite some time, probably since he left the treatment facility, but unbeknownst to him and to us all, his mental illness was worsening. According to the doctor who examined him last night, this was further complicated by the onset of hyperacusis."

"Of what?" the mayor asked.

"It's a condition that results in extreme sensitivity to sounds. Noise became almost intolerable to him and the combination of these conditions, together with worsening psychosis, may have been what drove him to commit these murders."

"I see. Extraordinary. Unprecedented," the mayor said.

"He's been transferred to a psychiatric ward and will probably serve his life sentence in a security hospital where we can ensure he's no longer a danger to himself or others," Sheriff Jack concluded. Then, glancing at May, he continued. "This criminal was operating completely under the radar, and it was only thanks to the hard work and the intuitive skill of my deputy that he was arrested, and that the life of his next victim was saved. Otherwise, in that hidden cellar, he could have widened his scope and continued to break into homes and commit many more murders. Deputy Moore risked her life, and serious injury, to take him down."

Now, May felt even more nervous as the mayor swung around to stare at her.

"How are you feeling, Deputy?" he demanded.

"Fine, thanks, sir. Just a little sore throat," she said, surprised that he would even care, given his history of animosity towards her.

Sheriff Jack was looking at him in a slightly surprised way too, as if he couldn't quite believe that the mayor had actually asked after her.

The mayor took a deep breath.

May had a feeling that this was hard for him to say, because he seemed to be wrestling with himself briefly before letting the words out. She felt a stab of fear, anticipating that the inquiry after her health was just a formality and that there was going to be a "but" that sent her career smashing into smithereens.

But when he spoke again, she almost fell over in shock.

"I believe in giving credit where credit's due. I acknowledge the very important and crucial role that you played. And in particular, I want to thank you for saving the life of the latest victim."

"Thank you, Mayor Tillman. I was just doing my job," she told him humbly.

"A job well done. I commend you, and your department, for handling this case impeccably."

May blinked in astonishment. Mayor Tillman was thanking her! He was setting the bad blood aside—for now, at any rate. May knew that he still didn't like her. There was no way they were going to ever be friends. But for now, she had his official approval, and they were no longer enemies.

The mayor rose, nodded at all of them, then strode out of the office and out of the police department, with his entourage following.

As soon as he left, May felt as if a huge weight had been lifted off her shoulders.

As Sheriff Jack nodded proudly at her, May knew there was only one thing that could possibly make this surprising day any better. That was to get the news she longed for about that mysterious video of Lauren. But May knew she was going to have to be patient because that information might arrive in weeks or months, or perhaps not at all.

EPILOGUE

It was late that night, and May was in bed, at home, after a surprisingly pleasant dinner with her parents. They'd congratulated her on the case, and she'd given them a blow-by-blow account of it in her still-hoarse voice, all the way up to her struggle with the killer on the jetty.

She didn't want her mother upset by hearing how close May had come to losing her life. Instead, she'd glossed over that life and death battle, thanked her mother, and asked her to please thank Edna, because ultimately, her mother's suggestions and Edna's detailed historical input had provided the pivotal information to solve the case.

Local knowledge! May couldn't be more grateful for it.

Now, with her head on the pillow, she was on the point of sleep when her phone rang. She jumped, startled by the noise, and was suddenly wide awake when she saw it was Kerry on the line.

She grabbed up the call.

"Hey, Kerry."

"Hey, sis," Kerry sounded focused, as if she was on the warpath. "Listen, well done for the case. We heard about it. Excellent work. My bosses say the deductive process you followed was nothing short of genius. But that's not why I'm calling."

May sat up, pulling the covers back, her heart speeding up. This had to be the news she'd been waiting for. Kerry must have found something!

"The video," her sister said, getting straight to the point.

"What about it?" May's mouth felt dry. This was so important. It meant so much.

"I think I've found a lead."

"You have?" May felt a surge of complex emotion. Hope was the one that she felt the most strongly.

"The camera belongs to a woman called Harriet Downes."

"Harriet Downes?" May racked her brain. The name sounded vaguely familiar, but not recently so. And a woman? She'd expected that the perpetrator, if this was that person, would be a man.

"Yes. Harriet Downes. She posted other footage on social media. We were able to access it in the archives. That missing pixel is there, it's identical. It's like a signature."

May shivered at the thought.

"So, I need to find Harriet urgently?" she asked Kerry

"Well, there's a slight problem there, sis."

"What's that?" May asked, now worried.

"Harriet is apparently dead."

"What?" May asked, now breathless.

"She went missing about nine years ago. Presumed to be killed in an accident. But maybe she wasn't if she's still leaving footage on your computer. Maybe we need to check that and put out a search for her. She'd be thirty-three years old now."

May was breathing fast now. She was battling to take in the twists and complexity that lurked in this troubling case.

"Do you have any photos of her? How do we find her?"

Kerry sighed. "The best I can find are photos a couple of years before she disappeared. She doesn't have any family in the area. She seems to have moved here from Maine at the age of twenty after her mother died. And she'd look different now, more than ten years on."

"Is it going to be possible? It feels like we're hunting a ghost," May protested, anxiety flaring.

But Kerry confidently assured her, "Oh, yes. It will be possible, with the help of the very advanced software that the FBI has available. We'll be able to create a ten years on composite of what she's likely to look like, and we can put that out with an APB. We're going to find her, May."

Hearing the anger and resolve in her sister's tone strengthened May's own determination all over again. This was not over. And this woman would not just disappear, after being involved, somehow, in such atrocities.

"Let's do it," May said firmly. "You get the pics, I'll do the APB, and we'll hunt her down. Her time for hiding is over."

Working together, May hoped that they would find her, no matter what it took. Harriet Downes would no longer be a ghost.

And she would lead them to the answers they needed.

NOW AVAILABLE!

NEVER LET GO
(A May Moore Suspense Thriller—Book 9)

From #1 bestselling mystery and suspense author Blake Pierce comes a gripping new series: May Moore, 29, an average Midwestern woman and deputy sheriff, has always lived in the shadow of her older, brilliant FBI agent sister. Yet the sisters are united by the cold case of their missing younger sister—and when a new serial killer strikes in May's quiet, Minnesota lakeside town, it is May's turn to prove herself, to try to outshine her sister and the FBI, and, in this action-packed thriller, to outwit and hunt down a diabolical killer before he strikes again.

"A masterpiece of thriller and mystery."
—Books and Movie Reviews, Roberto Mattos (re Once Gone)

When a victim narrowly escapes from an eerie, underground bunker near the lake, May must race to decode who is behind the crime—and who else is out there, waiting to saved.

But as May goes deeper down the rabbit hole, she soon realizes this case—and this killer—are far more dangerous than they seem. And in the isolated Midwest outskirts, every horror is amplified.

Can she find this elusive killer before another victim vanishes underground?

A page-turning and harrowing crime thriller featuring a brilliant and tortured Deputy Sheriff, the MAY MOORE series is a riveting mystery, packed with non-stop action, suspense, jaw-dropping twists, and driven by a breakneck pace that will keep you flipping pages late into the night.

Future books in the series will be available soon!

"An edge of your seat thriller in a new series that keeps you turning pages! ...So many twists, turns and red herrings… I can't wait to see what happens next."
—Reader review (Her Last Wish)

"A strong, complex story about two FBI agents trying to stop a serial killer. If you want an author to capture your attention and have you guessing, yet trying to put the pieces together, Pierce is your author!"
—Reader review (Her Last Wish)

"A typical Blake Pierce twisting, turning, roller coaster ride suspense thriller. Will have you turning the pages to the last sentence of the last chapter!!!"
—Reader review (City of Prey)

"Right from the start we have an unusual protagonist that I haven't seen done in this genre before. The action is nonstop… A very atmospheric novel that will keep you turning pages well into the wee hours."
—Reader review (City of Prey)

"Everything that I look for in a book… a great plot, interesting characters, and grabs your interest right away. The book moves along at a breakneck pace and stays that way until the end. Now on go I to book two!"
—Reader review (Girl, Alone)

"Exciting, heart pounding, edge of your seat book… a must read for mystery and suspense readers!"
—Reader review (Girl, Alone)

Blake Pierce

Blake Pierce is the USA Today bestselling author of the RILEY PAGE mystery series, which includes seventeen books. Blake Pierce is also the author of the MACKENZIE WHITE mystery series, comprising fourteen books; of the AVERY BLACK mystery series, comprising six books; of the KERI LOCKE mystery series, comprising five books; of the MAKING OF RILEY PAIGE mystery series, comprising six books; of the KATE WISE mystery series, comprising seven books; of the CHLOE FINE psychological suspense mystery, comprising six books; of the JESSIE HUNT psychological suspense thriller series, comprising twenty six books; of the AU PAIR psychological suspense thriller series, comprising three books; of the ZOE PRIME mystery series, comprising six books; of the ADELE SHARP mystery series, comprising sixteen books, of the EUROPEAN VOYAGE cozy mystery series, comprising six books; of the new LAURA FROST FBI suspense thriller, comprising eleven books (and counting); of the new ELLA DARK FBI suspense thriller, comprising fourteen books (and counting); of the A YEAR IN EUROPE cozy mystery series, comprising nine books, of the AVA GOLD mystery series, comprising six books (and counting); of the RACHEL GIFT mystery series, comprising ten books (and counting); of the VALERIE LAW mystery series, comprising nine books (and counting); of the PAIGE KING mystery series, comprising eight books (and counting); of the MAY MOORE mystery series, comprising eleven books (and counting); the CORA SHIELDS mystery series, comprising five books (and counting); and of the NICKY LYONS mystery series, comprising five books (and counting).

An avid reader and lifelong fan of the mystery and thriller genres, Blake loves to hear from you, so please feel free to visit www.blakepierceauthor.com to learn more and stay in touch.

BOOKS BY BLAKE PIERCE

NICKY LYONS MYSTERY SERIES
ALL MINE (Book #1)
ALL HIS (Book #2)
ALL HE SEES (Book #3)
ALL ALONE (Book #4)
ALL FOR ONE (Book #5)

CORA SHIELDS MYSTERY SERIES
UNDONE (Book #1)
UNWANTED (Book #2)
UNHINGED (Book #3)
UNSAID (Book #4)
UNGLUED (Book #5)

MAY MOORE SUSPENSE THRILLER
NEVER RUN (Book #1)
NEVER TELL (Book #2)
NEVER LIVE (Book #3)
NEVER HIDE (Book #4)
NEVER FORGIVE (Book #5)
NEVER AGAIN (Book #6)
NEVER LOOK BACK (Book #7)
NEVER FORGET (Book #8)
NEVER LET GO (Book #9)
NEVER PRETEND (Book #10)
NEVER HESITATE (Book #11)

PAIGE KING MYSTERY SERIES
THE GIRL HE PINED (Book #1)
THE GIRL HE CHOSE (Book #2)
THE GIRL HE TOOK (Book #3)
THE GIRL HE WISHED (Book #4)
THE GIRL HE CROWNED (Book #5)
THE GIRL HE WATCHED (Book #6)
THE GIRL HE WANTED (Book #7)
THE GIRL HE CLAIMED (Book #8)

VALERIE LAW MYSTERY SERIES
NO MERCY (Book #1)
NO PITY (Book #2)
NO FEAR (Book #3)
NO SLEEP (Book #4)
NO QUARTER (Book #5)
NO CHANCE (Book #6)
NO REFUGE (Book #7)
NO GRACE (Book #8)
NO ESCAPE (Book #9)

RACHEL GIFT MYSTERY SERIES
HER LAST WISH (Book #1)
HER LAST CHANCE (Book #2)
HER LAST HOPE (Book #3)
HER LAST FEAR (Book #4)
HER LAST CHOICE (Book #5)
HER LAST BREATH (Book #6)
HER LAST MISTAKE (Book #7)
HER LAST DESIRE (Book #8)
HER LAST REGRET (Book #9)
HER LAST HOUR (Book #10)

AVA GOLD MYSTERY SERIES
CITY OF PREY (Book #1)
CITY OF FEAR (Book #2)
CITY OF BONES (Book #3)
CITY OF GHOSTS (Book #4)
CITY OF DEATH (Book #5)
CITY OF VICE (Book #6)

A YEAR IN EUROPE
A MURDER IN PARIS (Book #1)
DEATH IN FLORENCE (Book #2)
VENGEANCE IN VIENNA (Book #3)
A FATALITY IN SPAIN (Book #4)

ELLA DARK FBI SUSPENSE THRILLER
GIRL, ALONE (Book #1)
GIRL, TAKEN (Book #2)

GIRL, HUNTED (Book #3)
GIRL, SILENCED (Book #4)
GIRL, VANISHED (Book 5)
GIRL ERASED (Book #6)
GIRL, FORSAKEN (Book #7)
GIRL, TRAPPED (Book #8)
GIRL, EXPENDABLE (Book #9)
GIRL, ESCAPED (Book #10)
GIRL, HIS (Book #11)
GIRL, LURED (Book #12)
GIRL, MISSING (Book #13)
GIRL, UNKNOWN (Book #14)

LAURA FROST FBI SUSPENSE THRILLER
ALREADY GONE (Book #1)
ALREADY SEEN (Book #2)
ALREADY TRAPPED (Book #3)
ALREADY MISSING (Book #4)
ALREADY DEAD (Book #5)
ALREADY TAKEN (Book #6)
ALREADY CHOSEN (Book #7)
ALREADY LOST (Book #8)
ALREADY HIS (Book #9)
ALREADY LURED (Book #10)
ALREADY COLD (Book #11)

EUROPEAN VOYAGE COZY MYSTERY SERIES
MURDER (AND BAKLAVA) (Book #1)
DEATH (AND APPLE STRUDEL) (Book #2)
CRIME (AND LAGER) (Book #3)
MISFORTUNE (AND GOUDA) (Book #4)
CALAMITY (AND A DANISH) (Book #5)
MAYHEM (AND HERRING) (Book #6)

ADELE SHARP MYSTERY SERIES
LEFT TO DIE (Book #1)
LEFT TO RUN (Book #2)
LEFT TO HIDE (Book #3)
LEFT TO KILL (Book #4)
LEFT TO MURDER (Book #5)
LEFT TO ENVY (Book #6)

LEFT TO LAPSE (Book #7)
LEFT TO VANISH (Book #8)
LEFT TO HUNT (Book #9)
LEFT TO FEAR (Book #10)
LEFT TO PREY (Book #11)
LEFT TO LURE (Book #12)
LEFT TO CRAVE (Book #13)
LEFT TO LOATHE (Book #14)
LEFT TO HARM (Book #15)
LEFT TO RUIN (Book #16)

THE AU PAIR SERIES
ALMOST GONE (Book#1)
ALMOST LOST (Book #2)
ALMOST DEAD (Book #3)

ZOE PRIME MYSTERY SERIES
FACE OF DEATH (Book#1)
FACE OF MURDER (Book #2)
FACE OF FEAR (Book #3)
FACE OF MADNESS (Book #4)
FACE OF FURY (Book #5)
FACE OF DARKNESS (Book #6)

A JESSIE HUNT PSYCHOLOGICAL SUSPENSE SERIES
THE PERFECT WIFE (Book #1)
THE PERFECT BLOCK (Book #2)
THE PERFECT HOUSE (Book #3)
THE PERFECT SMILE (Book #4)
THE PERFECT LIE (Book #5)
THE PERFECT LOOK (Book #6)
THE PERFECT AFFAIR (Book #7)
THE PERFECT ALIBI (Book #8)
THE PERFECT NEIGHBOR (Book #9)
THE PERFECT DISGUISE (Book #10)
THE PERFECT SECRET (Book #11)
THE PERFECT FAÇADE (Book #12)
THE PERFECT IMPRESSION (Book #13)
THE PERFECT DECEIT (Book #14)
THE PERFECT MISTRESS (Book #15)
THE PERFECT IMAGE (Book #16)

THE PERFECT VEIL (Book #17)
THE PERFECT INDISCRETION (Book #18)
THE PERFECT RUMOR (Book #19)
THE PERFECT COUPLE (Book #20)
THE PERFECT MURDER (Book #21)
THE PERFECT HUSBAND (Book #22)
THE PERFECT SCANDAL (Book #23)
THE PERFECT MASK (Book #24)
THE PERFECT RUSE (Book #25)
THE PERFECT VENEER (Book #26)

CHLOE FINE PSYCHOLOGICAL SUSPENSE SERIES

NEXT DOOR (Book #1)
A NEIGHBOR'S LIE (Book #2)
CUL DE SAC (Book #3)
SILENT NEIGHBOR (Book #4)
HOMECOMING (Book #5)
TINTED WINDOWS (Book #6)

KATE WISE MYSTERY SERIES

IF SHE KNEW (Book #1)
IF SHE SAW (Book #2)
IF SHE RAN (Book #3)
IF SHE HID (Book #4)
IF SHE FLED (Book #5)
IF SHE FEARED (Book #6)
IF SHE HEARD (Book #7)

THE MAKING OF RILEY PAIGE SERIES

WATCHING (Book #1)
WAITING (Book #2)
LURING (Book #3)
TAKING (Book #4)
STALKING (Book #5)
KILLING (Book #6)

RILEY PAIGE MYSTERY SERIES

ONCE GONE (Book #1)
ONCE TAKEN (Book #2)
ONCE CRAVED (Book #3)
ONCE LURED (Book #4)

ONCE HUNTED (Book #5)
ONCE PINED (Book #6)
ONCE FORSAKEN (Book #7)
ONCE COLD (Book #8)
ONCE STALKED (Book #9)
ONCE LOST (Book #10)
ONCE BURIED (Book #11)
ONCE BOUND (Book #12)
ONCE TRAPPED (Book #13)
ONCE DORMANT (Book #14)
ONCE SHUNNED (Book #15)
ONCE MISSED (Book #16)
ONCE CHOSEN (Book #17)

MACKENZIE WHITE MYSTERY SERIES
BEFORE HE KILLS (Book #1)
BEFORE HE SEES (Book #2)
BEFORE HE COVETS (Book #3)
BEFORE HE TAKES (Book #4)
BEFORE HE NEEDS (Book #5)
BEFORE HE FEELS (Book #6)
BEFORE HE SINS (Book #7)
BEFORE HE HUNTS (Book #8)
BEFORE HE PREYS (Book #9)
BEFORE HE LONGS (Book #10)
BEFORE HE LAPSES (Book #11)
BEFORE HE ENVIES (Book #12)
BEFORE HE STALKS (Book #13)
BEFORE HE HARMS (Book #14)

AVERY BLACK MYSTERY SERIES
CAUSE TO KILL (Book #1)
CAUSE TO RUN (Book #2)
CAUSE TO HIDE (Book #3)
CAUSE TO FEAR (Book #4)
CAUSE TO SAVE (Book #5)
CAUSE TO DREAD (Book #6)

KERI LOCKE MYSTERY SERIES
A TRACE OF DEATH (Book #1)
A TRACE OF MURDER (Book #2)

A TRACE OF VICE (Book #3)
A TRACE OF CRIME (Book #4)
A TRACE OF HOPE (Book #5)

CPSIA information can be obtained
at www.ICGtesting.com
Printed in the USA
LVHW051927240523
747940LV00004B/54

9 781094 379791